Daisy gaped but the silence was only temporary. "What I want from a man is utterly beyond your comprehension, I'm sure. Your cold, passionless mind could not begin to understand my need for companionship or affection."

Max was offended by her accusation. "You believe I lack passion?"

She glared at him. "Yes, I do! I doubt you know what to do with a woman, you poor man."

His honor was at stake now.

Passionless? Cold? Hardly!

Max closed the distance between them, bent Miss Ellis over his arm, and planted a long kiss on her pretty pink lips to prove her wrong.

It was not a subtle kiss, nor was it brief. He'd been celibate for years because of her. And since she insisted he was no longer her guardian, he could be the scoundrel he used to be.

The characters and events portrayed in this book are fictitious. Any similarity to real persons, living or dead, is purely coincidental and not intended by the author.

MISS ELLIS UNLEASHED © 2025 by Heather Boyd
ISBN: 978-1-922733-47-4
Editing by Kelli Collins

All rights reserved. No part of this book may be reproduced in any form by any electronic or mechanical means—except in the case of brief quotations embodied in critical articles or reviews—without written permission of the author.

Heather Boyd
USA TODAY BESTSELLING AUTHOR

Miss Ellis Unleashed

Chapter One

DAISY ELLIS FLINCHED as the front door of her Golden Square home slammed shut. She gritted her teeth as heavy male footsteps disturbed her peaceful morning yet again. Her guardian, Lord Throsby—an irritable viscount—rushed past the sitting room doorway before his steps faded away toward the rear of the house.

Another door slammed shut, and all fell silent again.

The housekeeper, Mrs. Lamb, quietly set aside her sewing and rose from her nearby chair. "Lord Throsby is back earlier than usual," she murmured, eyes on the door to the hall. She primped her hair absently. "I'd best see if he needs anything."

Daisy rolled her eyes. Her friend Gabby, the Duchess of Mamble, sighed softly as the housekeeper slipped from the room.

Even though the housekeeper was a decade and older than Throsby, Mrs. Lamb had developed a rather transparent soft spot for the surly viscount.

Daisy remained at the table, refusing to become interested in his activities. "No doubt he will think of something she can do for him. Throsby is nothing if not predictable," she said to her esteemed guest.

Gabby smothered a laugh. "Indeed he is."

"He will charge about, call for his valet, change his

clothes but depart the house within twenty minutes, ten if we are extremely fortunate," Daisy confessed in a whisper.

"That is how my Sebastian is. Rush, rush, all the time, but every now and then he stops to linger at my side."

"I should hope so," Daisy answered. "A wife is worth lingering over, especially when they are as lovely as you."

Gabby's cheeks turned pink with a blush. She and the duke were a passionate couple, madly in love, and the duke was not ashamed to prove his interest, no matter where the couple found themselves.

Daisy might have enjoyed a similar devotion, had the viscount gotten out of her way.

She *wished* her stuffy guardian would leave her side. She and Throsby had never gotten along. But everyone else, from the housekeeper down to the boot boy, seemed to tolerate his presence.

Daisy could not understand why.

The man was a menace to her peace.

Before he went out again today, he would poke his stern face through the sitting room doorway and look about the space for any signs of wickedness she might be involved in. He'd demand to know what she'd been doing all morning, as if she could not help but get into great mischief during his brief absences. It was hardly likely she'd have been properly seduced with her best friend in the room—a servant, too—or when he had been gone barely half an hour.

Daisy picked up the news sheet lying neglected on the table and shook it out. Though she was almost too excited to sit still, and certainly there was nothing of consequence in it to warrant a second perusal, she started to read the paper out loud to Gabby.

Daisy had spent the last half hour discussing the fun she would have tonight. But it was the promise of *tomorrow* that occupied her thoughts even more.

Tomorrow would be Daisy's first day as an independent woman. The guardianship she'd chafed under for four years ended tonight at the stroke of midnight.

Daisy had nothing special planned to celebrate her twentieth birthday other than doing as she pleased at last. After tonight, Throsby would have no power to complain if she misbehaved anymore.

And by misbehaving, she meant simply laughing and having a jolly good time.

She poured another cup of tea for Gabby and topped up her own cup too, smiling to herself, and then continued to recite the paper as her guardian's footsteps inevitably sounded through the house once more.

Throsby rushed everywhere. Inside the house—but never upstairs, thankfully—and out in society, too. Daisy's head spun some nights at the speed in which he made her circle the ballrooms at the entertainments he decided she must attend.

Today, he must have paused only a few minutes to change into fresh clothing. He must be late for an appointment or something equally dull, not that she cared enough to inquire what he was up to.

She preferred to know little about her guardian, especially since he hardly expressed an interest in her opinion. The only kindness he'd ever shown her was allowing Daisy to mourn her father in private before finally bringing her out at nineteen years of age. A little later than most debutants perhaps, but she hadn't been ready to make merry before that.

The season had been fun so far, making new friends, and, in the beginning, her interest in gentlemen and finding a husband had been genuine. But the gentlemen she admired were often not the marrying kind. She accepted that her smaller dowry made her less interesting as a potential bride, and her disinterest in men who valued money over love had grown in leaps and bounds.

Daisy still liked to look at handsome men, to admire them, and to imagine the advantages of choosing one man over the other for her husband.

Unfortunately, once many fellows opened their mouths, beyond pleasantries, she discovered only self-absorbed scoundrels who cared nothing for hearing her opinion, or any other woman's, for that matter. The best men were often already married, like her friend Gabby's husband, Sebastian, Duke of Mamble.

Now, *there* was a man who appreciated an intelligent woman.

Throsby had managed to chase away those who were left, glowering like the beast he had always been because they did not meet with *his* approval.

As if summoned by her thought, the viscount burst into the room without knocking, but after four years, Daisy was prepared for such interruptions. She did not look up and complain about his lack of manners. A true gentleman would have knocked, but her guardian deemed himself above such things. Besides, what would be the point of complaining now? It was the last day he could ever attempt to catch her ignoring the rules of proper society with a suitor who had slipped past his guard.

He sputtered, caught by surprise by the presence of a duchess at Daisy's side. "Oh, forgive me, your grace, I was not informed you were visiting."

Gabby stood. "I was just on my way home again, Lord Throsby. Until tomorrow, Daisy."

Daisy sighed, disappointed that Gabby's visit was to be shorter than her last.

She said goodbye to her friend and watched her waltz out of the room. Daisy resumed her interest in the paper as if the viscount wasn't there.

"I did not mean to interrupt," he murmured.

"Think nothing of it," Daisy answered in an offhand way meant to convey that he surely had.

He cleared his throat loudly to get her attention. "Any other callers of note today?"

She cocked her head to the side, annoyed by the question that surely had to be about potential suitors, and turned the page. "The king called to ask for my hand in marriage. Gabby thinks I should accept."

Throsby scoffed. "The king is already married and not presently in London. You both know that."

Throsby's sense of humor had always been deficient. She closed her eyes and easily imagined his expression right now. He would be wearing a scowl. He always did. Just as he always wore a pristine white shirt, and a navy-blue coat and waistcoat over fawn breeches at this time of day.

His face would be clean-shaven, his hair cut too short, and a plain pocket watch and chain would be draped just above his waist. Understated, night and day. That was her guardian. The man did nothing to draw attention to himself. He was the sort of man women barely looked at twice.

Throsby cleared his throat again. "Will you ever be done with that paper?"

"I assure you I am reading as fast as I can," she promised him.

"With your eyes closed?"

Daisy glanced up at him. Yes, he was exactly as she'd imagined. The man never changed. Throsby was positively glowering at her, too, and Daisy's satisfaction in the day increased to see that reaction. She rather enjoyed upsetting Throsby morning noon and night.

She smiled slowly but out of habit rather than fondness for the viscount looming over her. "They were not closed. I was concentrating."

Throsby snorted but did not call her a liar outright. He was undoubtedly thinking it, though.

Over the years of the guardianship, Daisy had developed a remarkable desire to annoy this man and had discovered what irritated him most of all was a lack of interest in complying with his demands.

Appearing to take all day to read the news sheet was just one of a number she routinely employed to irk him. She took great delight in unsettling him with her other quiet rebellions, too. The best was adjusting her garter in front of him and flashing her stocking-covered ankle. She reserved that for dire emergencies, when she wanted Throsby to leave the house in a tearing hurry.

The viscount appeared easily flustered by a glimpse of stocking, especially hers.

Daisy returned to reading the paper again, but she was

aware of the viscount's lingering presence, his huff of annoyance, and his tight grip on the door handle.

The man needed a woman to rid him of all that pent-up tension.

But Throsby had never courted anyone while he'd been her guardian, even when she had conspired to throw a lonely widow directly into his path. The man had stuck to her side like glue for the whole of the season so far, too. But that was all about to end tonight.

She wanted to laugh and shout out her impatience for that moment to come.

Instead, she exhaled softly. "Did you want something else from me, my lord?" She asked the question innocently enough...but she glanced up at him from beneath her lashes while simultaneously leaning down to check if her garter needed adjustment.

The viscount clenched his jaw and resolutely refused to look at what she was doing to her leg. "I'm to meet the Duke of Mamble today at the club for luncheon."

"Yes, Gabby told me all about it. And it's a Tuesday, so you always go out today."

"There was something I wanted to show him from today's paper," he grumbled.

"But I'm not done with reading it yet," she protested, eyes wide with feigned surprise. "What a shame you denied me my own copy so you have to share yours."

She said it mildly enough but inside, she was still seething mad at him for never letting her have her own. He claimed the expense was excessive when they could share.

"Never mind the paper now," he said, sighing heavily afterward. "I'll purchase another copy on my way there."

Daisy shrugged. "Well, good, and have a jolly good time out with your friends."

"The Mambles are your friends, not mine." Throsby's lips thinned briefly, but when Daisy inched her gown up again, he shook his head. "I will return in plenty of time to escort you to tonight's masquerade."

"It will never be said that you have shirked your duty as a guardian, my lord," she murmured, picking up the paper again but stealing a glance at his face first. There was no indication of anticipation for their last ball together or for escorting her there. Yet, he was hesitating to leave. Would she have to throw her gown up over her knees today to drive him away?

Daisy had always assumed Throsby was as eager as herself for an end to their annoying and unnecessary arrangement, but lately, he seemed to linger around as if she needed constant supervision.

Daisy had lost her papa at sixteen years old but had managed the household and her papa's finances for many years before that. She'd hardly needed a guardian to manage so small a sum of money, and certainly not a man like Throsby. He'd been a complete stranger when he had arrived and had taken over everything, despite her protests that she was more than capable and she did not need him.

And it continued to irk her that her papa had saddled her with a humorless lump of a man. Papa's final act as a father had been hard to reconcile.

She squinted at the paper and mumbled a few sentences softly, pretending she didn't fully comprehend what she read, since that too would irk him.

Throsby snorted again. "So, I will be waiting for you at

eight o'clock in the hall," he announced as the housekeeper slipped into the room around him.

"Yes, and I will be ready and on time as you expect me to be," she answered, knowing some sort of response was required to complete what had become their daily ritual.

When she said nothing more, he left the room as abruptly as he'd come, and the front door slammed shut behind him.

Daisy tossed the paper aside in disgust and looked around the cluttered room.

Just a few more hours and then…freedom.

Her home would be her own again, she could spread out her belongings, and her servants would take *her* orders and not his. And she would have the distinct pleasure of having *her* servants move her father's old bed back upstairs to the currently empty master chamber where it should have remained all along.

There would be no more pleasing Lord Throsby's needs under this roof.

Daisy sighed as the housekeeper sat at her side once more.

Some supervision *was* required from time to time, though. She wasn't completely immoral.

"You can come out now, Mr. Pinkerton," Daisy called, and then flipped up the long cloth covering the table and peeked under. "He'll be gone for five and forty minutes at the very least."

"I thought he'd never leave," Pinkerton replied, as he emerged from under the table. He straightened his coat, smoothed his hair, and cast a cheeky smile toward the housekeeper. "That was close. I was certain he'd find me this time around. I don't know why he doesn't like me."

Vain, pretty men—fops—seemed to bother the viscount excessively when they came to call. Honestly, she couldn't work out why the man bothered him so much, either. Pinkerton was amusing but hardly a suitor. He'd never once taken liberties anytime he hid under the table, either, and his gaze only ever lingered on other men, and never her own cleavage or legs.

"Never mind Throsby. I am eager to hear about your recent travels abroad…and that handsome man you met along the way," she promised, as she uncovered the map she had hidden inside the paper. Talk of her traveling anywhere beyond London did seem to alarm Throsby excessively. "I've always wanted to travel to Rome, too, no matter how tedious Throsby claims I would find it."

Chapter Two

Miss Daisy Ellis had been a thorn in Max's side since the day they'd met. He'd been stuck with her as his ward for several years, and tomorrow, he would finally be free of the infernal arrangement. No more mincing his words, pretending her future, her good reputation, was the only thing that mattered in his entire life.

He glanced down at the top of her head—dark curls adorned with silly ribbons and flower buds yet again—and withheld a heavy sigh.

Miss Ellis appeared serene, as if his company did not bother her, which meant the minx was plotting some secret excursion he would not approve of, like almost everything she did. Her attempts to consort with the rakes and rogues who routinely called on her behind his back—or men so timid they would hide beneath a table, for God's sake, whenever he was about—had mostly been routed by servants he paid well to protect her from ruin.

The minx hid her penchant for mischief from others well, but he knew the signs of trouble in the wind. She was too agreeable with him tonight, smiling too often in that empty-headed way she'd adopted of late. No matter what he said or how hard he scowled, she never stopped. Not a word of complaint had left her lips for the past two hours, and that was always an omen of trouble on the horizon.

He nodded to an unmarried marquess as he staggered past, too deep in his cups for decent conversation, and thankfully, the rogue thought better of stopping to flirt with his ward and ogle her chest.

Word had spread quite early into his guardianship that, despite his prior reputation for scandalous misadventures himself, Max would brook no nonsense when it came to his ward's future. But still, some fools came to call on her when he was gone from the house with that goal in mind.

His only amusement was that Miss Ellis hid the swains in some of the most awkward places about the house, and they still came back for more.

He wanted the minx respectably wed, not ruined during the guardianship, even though her father's instructions had been quite vague in that regard. But Max had a code he followed when it came to innocents. The household staff had strict orders to watch over her when he was out and report any caller to him immediately after he returned.

To date, most of the fellows he was close acquaintances with had valued their continued freedom and their friendship with him and behaved. While polite to Miss Ellis in public, they had thankfully given her a wide berth at other times. However, some of the younger fellows new to Town hadn't heard about his expectations…but soon learned their lesson after a brief and pointed discussion of the benefits of owning a good pair of dueling pistols or swords.

Perhaps he had done her a disservice by being so strict with her suitors, but he knew the way men thought about women deep down. If a fellow could flirt and seduce without a thought for the consequences, they certainly would give it a try.

He should know. He'd been just like them once.

He and his friends, Lord Abelton and other, less polished rakes, had thoroughly enjoyed all the delights of London away from proper society until the wee hours of the morning since coming of age, and even before that.

But the guardianship had reformed Max, at least temporarily, and while his friends continued to chase skirts in low places, gamble, and imbibe freely, he had chosen abstinence and the pursuit of respectability. He mingled in high society for Daisy's sake, as if he'd always been an essential part of the *ton*.

Though he easily remembered being barred from balls early on, after disgracing himself in any number of settings by his drunkenness and flirtations.

Yes, the guardianship had changed him in many ways. He cared more about a lady's prospects than he ever had before. Nothing was amusing about a man leading a virginal woman astray, but most men viewed it as a challenge.

Not that Daisy Ellis would probably voice much of an objection if the right rogue came along. He'd overheard a few of her private conversations with her friends and saw the twinkle in her eye when she'd openly admired men across the room. He probably understood her better than anyone, something she would not care to hear, and that was why he continued to be so strict about propriety.

Daisy deserved a respectable marriage, and setting a good example might be the only way. It was for her own good, and for his peace of mind, too.

He could not hand her off to just any scoundrel.

Not like her father had done with *him*.

To this day, he still did not comprehend why Jonas Ellis,

a man he'd met once while drunk in a pleasure house, had decided Max was just the person to stand in a father's place after his death.

Of course, at the time they'd met, Max had not understood the older man was dying. He lasted all of three months after that first inauspicious conversation, and the arrival of a solicitor with documents was the first Max knew of any guardianship for the unknown daughter.

That was the first Miss Ellis had heard of Max and the guardianship, too, when she'd been dragged to his door. He'd narrowly missed being struck by a poorly aimed vase as her rage overflowed her good sense at their first meeting.

She'd stopped throwing things almost immediately after he promised to send her home again, but still wept over a father who'd left her a pauper in Max's charge. Over the next four years, Max had improved her finances to a degree that made her comfortably dowered but not by any means rich. The frost between them, though, had never thawed.

With the ball well underway, he was counting the minutes until they could leave. Daisy had danced twice, she'd whispered to several gentlemen she'd met before, made them laugh, and brought a twinkle to their eyes. Since it was still up to him for one more day to guard her reputation, he'd scowled until those fellows had slunk away again. Those men would never have honorable intentions toward someone like Daisy, someone without pots of money to fund their excesses or connections to elevate their family. He refused to see her heartbroken when they inevitably disappointed her.

He'd endured enough of her tears over her wastrel father's demise and what she saw as his betrayal to allow more heartbreak under his own watch.

But after tomorrow, he would leave all the bothersome guardian business behind and let her servants deal with any roguish encroachment. He'd trained them well. What happened to Daisy after that was none of his business, though he had the occasional nightmare about what the young woman's future could entail, once Miss Ellis was unleashed upon society.

However, he could not help looking forward to his own freedom, and a return to true unencumbered bachelorhood. His London town house was waiting. The new suits he'd ordered to wear had already arrived, and although he would only have limited staff to begin with, he was looking forward to having the ability to come and go at his own schedule once more and to entertain.

Abelton, his best friend and neighbor since childhood, had decided that a month-long celebration was in order, in honor of his release from what the man claimed was cruel servitude, and Max was keen for it as well.

Eventually, Daisy turned to him. "I should like to go home now, my lord."

He glanced at his pocket watch. "So early? It's not even midnight."

"Yes, I know. I'll speak to our hostess and tell her I'm not feeling the best. She'll understand."

"Are you ill?" he asked, instantly concerned. The last thing he wanted was to leave an unwell young woman in the hands of only servants to supervise her recovery.

"I'm fine." She put her hand on her belly and her cheeks colored. "Just a bit of pain."

He nodded quickly and did not ask for further clarification of what must surely be a woman's complaint, though that certainly explained her odd mood tonight, as well.

He followed at a distance as Daisy bid goodbye to the hostess, and then accompanied her outside when his carriage arrived. He was glad to be done with such stuffy balls, to be honest, and the constant worry that Daisy would slip away to meet a suitor and be ruined on his last night as guardian.

He handed her into the carriage, and they sat in their usual silence for the journey home. It wasn't uncommon for them to go long periods without speaking to each other, and he enjoyed the silence while it lasted. It was preferable to hearing how much she disliked him, to be honest.

But he gasped as the tiny Ellis town house came into view, astonished to see that every window was brightly lit at this late hour. "What the devil is going on here?"

"I thought that would be obvious," Daisy said, rudely shoving him back into his seat to exit the carriage first. "It's my birthday."

She shrieked and ran up the stairs like a little girl without a hint of propriety. He followed, irritated by her enthusiasm for running and for leaving him behind, too.

The birthday festivities *he'd* planned meticulously for her were not meant to start until luncheon tomorrow. He had it all organized, and the servants assured him everything was in order for a leisurely luncheon, followed by a night at the opera, about which he'd sworn her closest friends to secrecy.

But now, hours too early, the town house was abuzz with activity that he did not approve of. He stormed inside, cross at finding that, despite the late hour, servants rushed to and fro moving things about, and some even went out to the street—their arms full of objects he belatedly recognized as his own.

"Why is my writing slope being put into our carriage?" He rushed to the door after them and yelled, "Bring that back immediately."

"They won't listen. The servants no longer answer to you, Throsby," Daisy called out. "It's my birthday, and that means you don't have *any* authority here. Not over the servants and certainly not over me."

"The guardianship ends tomorrow," he reminded her.

"The guardianship papers say, strictly speaking, that you are my guardian *until* my twentieth birthday. That means at the stroke of midnight—the time of my birth, by the way—you can only be a visitor to this household, and your time is up."

He gaped at her.

"As you've always stressed, details are so important. A woman must guard her reputation against gentlemen who overstay their welcome. I'm sure you understand my position."

He narrowed his eyes. "*This* was what you were planning all night!"

"All month, actually. I had a little chat with the family solicitor and my friends, and they interpret the guardianship the way I do. And a particularly unpleasant discovery was finding out that, despite what you insinuated to me and others, there was never any requirement for my guardian to move into this house with me. In fact, there were a great many embellishments to the guardianship enacted by you that were unnecessary."

He gulped. "Damn that solicitor. He was trouble from the start."

"Because he was honest?"

"Ha," Max exclaimed. "That's laughable. First, he dipped handsomely into your father's pocket for years, depleting the estate by degrees, overcharging, and then inviting himself round for tea, only to stay for dinner too. Leech."

Daisy gaped. "That's not true. He's my friend."

"Has he spoken of his plans to marry you yet? I'm sure he will broach the subject as soon as I'm gone. I've already refused his suit once."

Daisy set her hands on her hips and glared at him. "He is just a friend. More than you have ever tried to be. You must leave this house immediately, lest my reputation be compromised and I have to marry someone as dull and rule-bound as you."

He growled low in his throat at the order, and took a menacing step toward her. "I can assure you the last thing I would ever do is marry someone as silly and vain as you turned out to be."

Daisy glared back, all appearance of the meek and mild debutant society knew finally vanishing from her face. "I'm glad we understand each other."

"Oh, we do indeed."

Miss Ellis smoothed down her skirts and curtsied.

But Max was too offended by the manner of his dismissal to offer her the same courtesy and bow. He'd had some idea she'd despised him, but not *this* much. To turn him out in the middle of the night was a slap in the face, especially after all the work he'd done to improve her fortune. But clearly in her eyes, he'd overstayed his pitiful welcome already.

So much for the special birthday celebration he'd planned for tomorrow to celebrate the end of the guardianship. At his expense, no less. Well, he'd celebrate it with his friends instead—and celebrate well into the night without her now.

He turned away and headed for the door.

"Goodbye, Lord Throsby," she called. "Don't let the door hit you on your way out," she added softly. "I would hate to have you tumble down the stairs and break something."

He heard her glee. Her transparent desire for a misfortune to befall him as he left.

Max stopped dead in his tracks, almost across the threshold. They'd always rubbed each other the wrong way, and he'd bit his tongue every single time they'd argued to spare himself her tears and flying vases. However, given the manner of his dismissal, he could not let further insult to his honor stand.

She ought to be taken down a peg or two—but not publicly, of course. That would never do, because she might retaliate in kind and damage her reputation. Besides, he would be more than happy to give her a private set down. He had a litany of complaints to unburden himself of.

And they were alone for the very last time for him to do so.

He pivoted to face Daisy Ellis, and saw her smug smile drop off her face in an instant. "I'm sure nothing of yours has been forgotten," she hastened to say.

He'd bet she'd written out lists of everything he owned long ago. And while he'd been doing his duty at yet another dull society ball as her guardian, for her benefit, her minions—the servants he'd placed his trust in all these years—had been hard at work evicting him.

He began to remove his gloves, one finger at a time.

"Miss Ellis, I did the best for you in a difficult situation. What should I have done with a grieving young girl, suddenly thrust into my life? Abandon her? Ignore her, like her father had? Take her away from everything she'd ever known?" He dropped one glove to the floor and started on the next as he took a step in her direction. "I never asked for this. Yet you show no gratitude for the sacrifices I've made. Ungrateful wretch. No doubt you'll ruin yourself with the first idiot who gets you alone, or that sniveling solicitor will get you in the end. All I did was delay the inevitable, I suppose."

Her mouth opened in shock. "How dare you!"

"Isn't that why you hate having a guardian? Did I spoil your fun by insisting you follow the rules of proper society so you could marry a man better than your father ever was? But you were never serious about finding a husband, were you?"

"You only wanted to be rid of me," she shrieked. "You never even asked if I wanted a husband!"

He flung his second glove away and stared down at her. "I've heard enough of you and your friends talking to know what you dream of when it comes to men. Any handsome fool with a pulse will do for a seduction, it seems."

Daisy gaped but the silence was only temporary. "What I want from a man is utterly beyond your comprehension, I'm sure. Your cold, passionless mind could not begin to understand my need for companionship or affection."

He was offended by her accusation. "You believe I lack passion?"

She glared at him. "Yes, I do! I doubt you know what to do with a woman, you poor man."

Max's honor was at stake now.

Passionless? Cold? Hardly!

He closed the distance between them, bent Miss Ellis over his arm, and planted a long kiss on her pretty pink lips to prove her wrong.

It was not a subtle kiss, nor was it brief. He'd been celibate for years because of her. And since she insisted he was no longer her guardian, he could be the scoundrel he used to be.

Daisy Ellis had never known the kind man he really was. He'd reformed for *her* sake. Kept back details of his life that might shock her. He'd given her no reason to doubt his character since the guardianship had started.

He softened the kiss and encouraged her lips to part, and although Daisy seemed surprised, he couldn't help but notice she didn't push him away either. When her tongue brushed against his, and her arms stretched up to embrace him, he knew he'd have to stop soon. Her soft moan of excitement had given him the vindication he sought.

This was passion, this was scandalous…and everything his days and nights had lacked since meeting her.

Max held her away from him, noting her dazed expression with immense satisfaction, then let her go. She seemed completely overcome and unable to find any more words to even scold him for taking liberties as she gaped at him.

Max bowed with an unnecessary flourish and faced her

one last time. Well-kissed and shocked suited her very much. "Farewell, Miss Ellis. I wish you all the luck in the world for your future."

And with that, he swept out the front door, satisfied in a way he'd not been in years, and squeezed into his carriage, surrounded by his possessions.

He'd bested the maddening creature at last. He was not without passion. And thanks to Daisy Ellis, his return to bachelorhood was off to an outstanding start.

Chapter Three

"I must compliment you, Miss Ellis," Mr. Pinkerton announced suddenly.

She raised a brow. "Must you again, sir?"

"You are a vision in green," he enthused, complimenting her choice of gown for the third time tonight.

"Why thank you," she answered modestly, snapping out her fan. Behind it, Daisy's face grew warm, made uncomfortable with hearing such excessive flattery uttered in the middle of a ballroom. She was not so obsessed about her looks that she sought such praise from her friends. She was not vain, or silly...despite Throsby's claim one month ago.

Pinkerton gestured around them. "The other ladies are pretty enough, and Miss Dawes particularly so, but none can compare to you," he said. "Don't you agree, Freddie?"

"I do indeed," Mr. Fredrickson replied, aiming a faint smile in her direction.

Daisy winced as Pinkerton continued to praise her over the top of her head to his good friend Fredrickson, whose only interest was the movement of Pinkerton's mouth. The pair had taken to singling her out at balls for conversation of late. Making her a party to their scandalous romance.

She hated this sort of behavior though, the false flattery grated, as did the continued demonizing of other women and her former friend, Miss Justine Dawes.

Since their friendship had ended a month ago, several male acquaintances kept attempting to suggest a rivalry existed between her and Miss Dawes. There was no rivalry on Daisy's side, only disappointment in her old friend's past silly behavior. Justine's sudden defection had taken her by surprise. She would not speak to Daisy now, or even make eye contact. Her attempts to avoid Daisy—and Gabby, too—were getting ridiculous.

Getting swept up in the pursuit of a husband was the only thing Daisy could accuse Justine of. She'd been desperate to make a match this season, more so than she'd ever let on, and had kept her pursuit of a gentleman that their friend Gabby had been interested in, as well, a secret. But Daisy also suspected Justine had been goaded to such behavior by her older sister, to make it a competition between them all as to who would marry first and best.

In the end, neither Justine nor Gabby had made a match with the particular gentleman they had favored, and only Gabby had gone on to make a grand match, and with a scandalous duke, no less. Someone Justine had spoken harshly about quite often.

Making a match was still very much on every debutant's mind, as the season had reached the midpoint, and it was occasionally on Daisy's, too. Even with a little more to offer in terms of a dowry than she'd assumed, Daisy had hoped to meet a man who she could love, and who could love her back without hesitation. She was anxiously waiting to meet him… but it would be neither of the men talking over the top of her head tonight.

She'd never felt so conflicted about what she wanted.

Everything had changed in the last month.

She excused herself but in a few steps, was confronted by another wide manly chest. She glanced up.

Mr. Ferris, a recently persistent caller at her home, was a young man she'd only met this season.

He smiled and slightly lowered himself so he did not tower over her so much. "Good evening, Miss Ellis, and may I say you look utterly bored tonight."

"I was," she admitted, laughing in relief that his comment wasn't a compliment. "Finally, a gentleman who speaks with some honesty."

The man grinned. "If it's honesty you seek, Miss Ellis, I'm just the man for the job. I have always regretted we have had so little chance to speak plainly, with so many servants constantly hovering about you at your home."

Daisy nodded. "As have I," she admitted, holding his gaze. Her servants refused to be dismissed whenever she had a gentleman come to call.

The man's smile grew wider. "I'm glad we're of the same mind. I trust we can dispense with the proprieties that only get in the way of a good time. Meet me in the library in five minutes, where we might improve our acquaintance by leaps and bounds."

Daisy's heart fluttered, but after a moment, she realized it was not with any sort of thrill at his invitation—because it had not been one. It was a demand to attend him. *Now.*

Daisy had thought herself free of bossy men, and a sense of foreboding crashed over her. Without the proprieties of polite society, many men turn into pigs. Private meetings with gentlemen were guaranteed to ruin a lady.

The other gents who called on her at home, who once hid from Throsby for a great lark, likely assumed that she was an easier target for seduction now, even with the housekeeper or footman in the room.

She wasn't so easily led astray as all that.

She was not some silly widgeon easily taken advantage of, as Throsby claimed!

When and if she married, it would be a considered decision on her part. Not the result of ruin.

Daisy glanced over her shoulder, only to be reminded that her nemesis was no longer there behind her and watching what she did.

She pasted a smile on her face as she regarded the latest man to disappoint her, and sighed. "I have promised a dance to Lord Abelton, and I could never disappoint him."

Lord Abelton was a jolly sort of fellow, utterly charming and disinterested in her for anything but dancing. He was a close friend of Throsby's, but she did not hold that against him. He used to smirk at Throsby whenever he said something dull, which made Daisy like the young lord more. He seemed a decent man, albeit a disinterested one.

Mr. Ferris had not been friends with Throsby at all, which was why Daisy had previously encouraged him to call. Ferris *had* expressed great delight upon hearing the guardianship had ended though, and he was transparently glad Throsby was out of her life once and for all.

She should have realized Ferris was a wolf in sheep's clothing, merely biding his time and manners to get her alone for what *he* wanted women for. Just as Throsby had warned her he might.

Mr. Ferris' eyes narrowed briefly, then he spun about to face the ballroom, watching the passing dancers. But his expression seemed strained now. He was annoyed with her.

"I'll wait," he said eventually.

Wait. Impatiently, no doubt, too. She groaned under her breath at the pickle she was in. She had thought Ferris was truly interested in her mind but, clearly, his ran to other parts of her body first.

Mr. Ferris would, unfortunately for him, be waiting all night long for Daisy to join him in the library. She could not afford to become embroiled in a scandal. And she did not believe Mr. Ferris considered a marriage between them when he'd demanded she meet him in the library.

Ferris abruptly took his leave and strutted around the perimeter of the dance floor.

She shook her head. Her interest in men had changed. They were confusing. Contrary. Often unfathomable. Even Throsby had turned out to be nothing like she expected.

When she met Abelton for their dance, something of her mood must have shown on her face because he raised a brow. "Is something wrong?"

"Nothing I cannot handle," she promised him with a smile.

He nodded, frowning though, and Daisy kept the smile on her face so that Abelton would not ask further questions.

In his arms, she relaxed enough to forget Mr. Ferris's demands, but she remained vexed with all other men. She sighed. "It does not take long for scoundrels to show their true colors, does it?"

"I suppose not. Word of the guardianship's end is slowly spreading through society, and soon you will be utterly besieged with improper offers from rakes and scoundrels," Abelton warned softly.

"It has already started," she grumbled. "Throsby must

have quite terrified them all before, because I seem to be looked upon very differently now."

"He did well then, as a guardian," Abelton suggested gently.

Perhaps he had.

And right now, Daisy felt almost hunted, although not for marriage.

Throsby had been right about so many things, unfortunately.

Father had left her finances in complete disarray, and if she hadn't read the ledgers from start to finish herself, she would not have learned what the viscount had done to improve her fortunes since taking control.

That improvement would not be enough to please any noble family, no matter if she was desperately loved for just herself. She might not marry into the aristocracy, as Throsby had always assumed she could. She had to lower her expectations further. A good match to a kind and affectionate gentleman was the best she could ever hope for. It was all she had ever truly wanted, really. To have a home and a family again. Someone who cared about her more than for the money she might bring them.

Throsby's parting words had spelled out in no uncertain terms the perilous nature of her position in society, the way no previous lecture from him ever had. He had even prepared her for the unpleasant and humiliating encounter with her solicitor when he had called and uttered an offer of marriage she'd immediately refused. The man had called twice since, assuming she'd eventually change her mind.

When her dance with Abelton ended, Daisy immediately went in search of her best friend, Gabby, the new Duchess of Mamble, in whose company she would remain safe from persistent scoundrels.

The duke and duchess were together across the room, Mamble in deep conversation with Lord Windermere. Gabby was hanging on Mamble's arm and laughing.

A new set was forming, forcing Daisy to wait before she could cross the dance floor to join them. But when she started out finally, she ran headlong into Justine Dawes.

She stopped and stared at her former friend.

Justine's gown was an exquisite shade of dark green that suited her complexion perfectly, but her eyes appeared red again, as they seemed to be every time their paths crossed lately. She looked wretchedly unhappy.

"Miss Dawes," she murmured quickly. "Are you unwell?"

"I am very well, thank you, Miss Ellis," Justine said stiffly, and then the usual awkward silence ensued as she lingered.

"I was just on my way to rejoin Gabby," Daisy announced.

"Yes, I'm sure you are wanted there," Justine answered with a hint of disapproval—or was it envy?

Daisy smiled and inclined her head. "Do enjoy your evening."

"And the same to you," Justine said, nodding back.

Daisy continued toward Gabby, troubled by the exchange. Sometimes, it felt like Justine wished to say more, even as she also couldn't wait to get away. There was a bitterness about her now that had never been apparent before...although that could be on account that her sister had wed the man Justine had pinned her hopes on marrying.

That newly matched pair was standing back to back across the room, too, talking to other guests rather than each other. Justine's sister had won herself a titled husband who didn't bother to hide the fact he didn't care for a wife who'd entrapped him into a humiliating public proposal.

Justine would have made him a better wife, had the sister not gotten in her way. Daisy wondered, and not for the first time, what Justine thought about that match. But likely she would never find out. Justine wouldn't be sharing further confidences with her anytime.

Gabby greeted Daisy warmly when she finally arrived at her side. "There you are."

"Yes, here I am," Daisy answered with a fond smile.

Gabby frowned. "I saw you in conversation with Miss Dawes just now."

"Yes. She did speak to me," Daisy admitted. Discussions about Justine never ended well between them, and she said no more.

Gabby's frown deepened. "What did she say to you tonight?"

"Nothing of note again."

The duchess pursed her lips, and after a moment, sighed. "You miss her."

Daisy shrugged. "Perhaps I do, but I'm no longer sure I ever knew her."

"I've felt the same for a while," Gabby whispered, glancing behind them. "I thought we'd all be friends forever."

"Forever is a very long time," Daisy murmured. "Nothing lasts."

Gabby grabbed her hand and squeezed it tightly. "You'll never be rid of me, I promise. We'll be sitting on the sidelines together, clutching our walking canes, watching our daughters and granddaughters set the ton on fire, and whispering of scandals well into our dotage."

Daisy laughed at the delightful picture she painted, but she wasn't so sure she'd have daughters or granddaughters invited to *ton* events like this anymore. Gabby was on a different path now than Daisy. She would forever have a life in high society.

She glanced around the room and found Justine was gone from the ballroom now. But then her eyes landed on Mr. Ferris, glowering at her from across the room, and she groaned under her breath. The scoundrel was a persistent devil.

His head tilted toward the library impatiently, but Daisy pretended not to see.

She glanced over her shoulder, and then quickly turned around again, blushing. She'd grown so accustomed to checking where Throsby stood when she attended balls like this, that the habit was still upon her. But Throsby was no longer near. He was no longer seen in proper society, either. He'd disappeared from her life as suddenly as he'd come, making her even more cross with him.

"I think Mr. Ferris is trying to catch your eye," Gabby whispered urgently.

Daisy kept a smile on her face. "He's very charming."

"As he's always been with you. But..." Gabby searched her face. "There's something wrong. Tell me."

Daisy quickly whispered the details of the scandalous invitation she'd received from Mr. Ferris tonight.

Gabby drew back, eyes widened in shock. "You cannot consider meeting with such a man here."

"I never planned to," Daisy promised, smiling at those around them who'd perhaps heard the panic in the duchess's tone, if not her exact words.

Gabby exhaled, her relief clear. "Mamble said he isn't in the market for a wife."

"Throsby already said as much," she murmured darkly.

"Has Mr. Ferris ever been so bold with you before?"

"No, but he's different without Throsby around. They all are. Gentlemen seem to have lost their manners around me, and I'm fast losing my patience with them, too."

Gabby sighed. "I'm so sorry. Bachelors can be beastly creatures. Well, until they fall in love and marry, that is."

"I always imagined husband-hunting would be more fun without Throsby around. I've discovered there were benefits to having a surly viscount standing behind me all the time, scowling at everyone. Although half the fun for me seemed to have been in alarming Throsby with what I might have done or agreed to do."

Gabby clucked her tongue. "Wasn't that a bit childish of you?"

"Yes, I suppose it was. Throsby wasn't interested in being my friend, not how your former guardian was to you. He…"

He confounded her, she was forced to admit. His continued absence from society was starting to alarm her, as well.

"My cousin Bennett was the exception, I now suspect, when it comes to guardians. But he was always my friend and had a great sense of humor and adventure. I miss him already, but he promised he will be with us for Christmas."

"Yes, you were luckier than I was in your guardian,"

Daisy said, biting back her growing sense of emptiness that had come after Throsby's departure from her life. "I haven't had a family to laugh with for a long time."

"You still have me," Gabby promised, hugging her close to her side. "Friends are as good as family."

That helped somewhat, but the emptiness remained. "Nothing is better than being the best friend of a duchess."

"We are in this together, and our friendship never depended on either of us tying the knot or being titled," Gabby reminded her, turning away abruptly as someone called her name.

Daisy stood about awkwardly beside Gabby, not excluded in the new conversation but not immediately part of it, either. Despite Gabby's reassurances that she belonged, navigating society as an independent woman was harder than she realized it would ever be. Her welcome was less certain.

Without Throsby—or perhaps it had been his title rather than the man—it seemed her appeal had taken a marked downturn except to scoundrels. Women who were once so keen to know her thoughts and opinions, while not turning away from her yet, now barely spared her a moment of their time anymore.

She'd resumed her position as a wallflower at society events without realizing it would happen so fast. It was only her close friendship with the Duchess of Mamble that kept her invited to dinners and balls like this.

Gabby eased closer again. "Why so great a sigh?"

"Just the usual despair I feel when being in society overwhelms me," she said, rather than admit she was feeling left behind.

Gabby chuckled. "I know what you mean, but try not to fret. There's a whole city to explore, and it's full of potential husbands. You never know where or when you will meet the right man."

Daisy sighed again. "Well, I know many men in higher society, and I want none of them—or they me, it seems—so far."

"You must be patient," Gabby warned, patting her hand. "Finding a husband is not easy. But you've always known what you wanted in a man. One with marriage on his mind first and without a care for the size of your fortune."

"Yes, that is true, and yet..." There was a problem. "I want something more," she whispered.

"Love?"

She blushed and then shrugged. "Perhaps I've become too particular."

"That's not true. You will find someone who cares about you and your reputation. Someone who watches over you, too."

"Now you're describing Throsby," she said sourly. "The last part, I mean."

"He was a difficult man, but that benefited you," Gabby whispered. "Throsby was reliable. You always knew what to expect from him."

She winced. *Not always.*

She had known to keep the details of her last conversation with Throsby to herself—and especially that astounding kiss of his, because Gabby would have imagined it meant something more. But what man kisses a woman like that and vanishes into thin air?

She shook her head. "On time and without any

embellishment whatsoever, just like the old, battered pocket watch he wore."

"You could know the time by how frequently he checked it at balls," Gabby giggled.

"Yes." But it was Throsby's parting words that played over in her head constantly since he'd disappeared from her life. "And he never boasted, even when he had every reason to."

"What could he boast about?"

"In four years, he somehow tripled the pitiful funds my father left to me," Daisy whispered.

"You only said he improved your fortune," Gabby murmured, looking at her with shock. "Tripled? Really? How did he do that?"

"With a great deal of hard work and dedication on his part, I suspect. I spent some time poring over the ledgers and papers he left behind, and I'm astonished by the degree of improvement."

"Your father would be pleased to know he made the right choice for your guardian then," Gabby whispered, squeezing her arm. "We'll talk of this more tomorrow when you come for luncheon. Please excuse me."

The duchess was pulled away into the arms of her grinning husband. They swept onto the dance floor, eyes locked on each other. So much in love.

Daisy sighed with happiness and looked away, but the group she'd been standing with broke apart, all going separate ways, leaving her standing by herself.

This was how she'd thought she'd wanted her life. Autonomy, and the freedom to do as she pleased. And yet she missed the way things had been before her friend had married...and before the guardianship had ended, too, for that matter.

When she had not been so alone.

Sometimes, she suspected her friendship with Gabby wouldn't outlast the season. Their interests were diverging, and there was not a thing to do to prevent it. The duke had many concerns that occupied his time, and they were now Gabby's, too. If Daisy were to marry someone the Mambles didn't care for, she might never see her friend again.

But, as things stood now, she was a wallflower again, and someone who might need to seek additional friendships. When she looked around, there were no friendly faces or invitations to join anyone's circle—not even Mr. Ferris remained in the room to pester her.

There was only the unsmiling and miserable Justine, watching proceedings from across the room once more, just like she was.

At the beginning of the season, Daisy had met Gabby and Justine by accident and forged strong bonds with them both, or so it seemed. Now, so far into the season, it felt awkward to seek an introduction to anyone else and expect more.

She pushed her anxiety down and headed for a chair among chaperones, where she could rest her aching feet. It was just her anxiety rearing its ugly head tonight. She belonged here within the *ton*. Even Throsby had said so. Only why did society feel so empty now?

Daisy had been seated for only a few minutes when Gabby rushed over and pulled her out of her chair, full of excitement for an invitation she'd just received. Daisy tried to feel the same level of enthusiasm. But it was a struggle when it became apparent that she would not be invited along with her friend.

So after supper, Daisy made up the excuse of a headache to leave the ball early and headed off alone in the duke's borrowed carriage.

Of all things, the expensive and vast comfort of the ducal carriage made her long for Throsby's cramped, simpler carriage...and even miss her surly former guardian's comforting silence at the end of a long evening.

Chapter Four

"Now that was a good bottle," Max enthused, regretfully setting his empty wine glass aside. He was at home in Hanover Square, where he could drink all night and sleep all day if he wanted to. And he had. Back in the old family pile, where he'd spent most of his life—both with his parents, and then without them for many years.

"There *was* another bottle left beside my chair earlier in the day," Lord Abelton murmured, stretching around his arms wide and searching in all directions beneath him, but finding nothing.

"I drank it after you were gone off to that ball," Max said, sorrowful for that fact. "The problem with drinking at all is that the bottles eventually run out."

"True. True," Abelton agreed, then he sat up swiftly and belched. "Can't believe you drank that bottle without me, though. It was my favorite."

"My apologies," Max said, although he wasn't really. The hours tended to blur together as the wine flowed freely. He had been celebrating his freedom for some time. Marking his return to bachelorhood in his previous drunken style with friends. It had been years since Max had slept on the lower floor of his town house beside an empty bottle, simply because he lacked the coordination to crawl his way upstairs to bed.

Max had been orphaned at a precocious twelve years of age, when his father had died suddenly in his sleep. He'd demanded to take care of himself, fighting distant relatives who had attempted to drag him off to the countryside, where they could tell him what to do while scheming to spend his money on stupid things.

Max had run away from them so often, they'd given up trying to bring him to heel—and left him and his fortune alone, too, claiming he'd beg them to take him back when he'd made a pauper of himself.

Those had been heady days, his absolute freedom as a youth alone in the city of London, and as he'd grown, he'd taken up drinking in earnest and gambling the nights away. Fortunately for him, he had an uncanny knack for winning more often than not. He'd grown his wealth steadily over the years, unlike his contemporaries, whose fortunes seemed always on the decline.

Over time, gambling had lost its appeal, and he'd turned his mind to the more complicated world of investment. He was older and wiser now. There was little he hadn't done in his life, and nothing much excited him anymore.

And he was well aware that he'd been going through the motions these last weeks, pretending to throw himself into his old life with abandon so that no one ever suspected his heart wasn't in the return to complete disorderly conduct so common in bachelors his age.

It was an adjustment, not having so many responsibilities and demands on his time. Much worse than he'd imagined. He was struggling to fill the hours when sober, so he drank excessively to pass the time.

Abelton bounced to his feet. "I danced with your girl tonight. Exquisite creature, as always."

"*Not* my girl," Max growled, correcting Abelton's assumption yet again. Ever since the guardianship had begun, Abelton had referred to Daisy Ellis as *Max's girl*. That couldn't have been further from the truth.

"I thought she looked a little forlorn, though. I saw that Ferris fellow drooling over her again, and her without a chaperone in sight. I swear I saw her flinch at something Ferris whispered to her."

Max locked his jaw around an oath and made himself shrug as if he didn't care. Daisy Ellis was none of his business. Not anymore. The only surprise was not hearing of the minx's ruin or a forced marriage already. He glanced at his timepiece. "Four o'clock. No, wait." He put the pocket watch up to his ear and listened. "I must have forgotten to wind it yesterday, and it's stopped again."

That hadn't happened in a long time.

"Never mind the time. It's still dark out, so we should do something," Abelton suggested with a grin. "I'm hungry."

"I could eat, too," Max decided, setting his hands under him and rising unsteadily. Food lessened the effect of all the wine he wasn't yet used to consuming.

Abelton could now drink him under the table. Once, he would not have stood a chance, but after years of good living on his part, Max was more concerned than impressed with Abelton's newfound tolerance. He'd hate to see the man drink himself to death. "I'll send for a servant to bring us something to eat."

"I think we need some company to go with the meal,"

Abelton said with a sly smile. "We could always call on *your girl*, you know. She could be home from that ball by now, in that empty house and feeling lonely."

Max sighed. Abelton loved nothing more than needling him about his former ward. Moving into her home had caused eyebrows to rise among his acquaintances, but he'd had good reason for that decision. He knew how painful it was when someone tried to rip you away from everything you'd ever known. He could not have kept her here in a strange house. The minx might have run away and something dreadful might have happened to her.

"Let's head to the club."

"Not to the club. Everyone there is so tedious these days. I've something special in mind for the pair of carefree bachelors we are tonight."

Max nodded slowly, curious for what Abelton intended but calling for his carriage to be readied and brought round front. Abelton needed everything to be exciting lately, and that was becoming exhausting, too.

The guardianship had mellowed Max more than he cared to admit, and he feared the change might just be fixed in stone. A nice night by the fire at the club with old friends, however tedious, or at home alone held greater appeal. But he didn't say so out loud. That's how he'd spent most of his evenings until very recently, and he missed that.

They loitered by his front windows, watching the carriages roll by, coming back from social events. As ever, Max's eyes were drawn in the direction of the Ellis town house, though he couldn't possibly see it from so far away.

He also missed Miss Ellis, much to his surprise.

He'd not spoken to her in weeks, and it still felt strange not to squabble with her every day. He shook off the worry thinking of her always inspired, lest Abelton notice and tease him about his continued concern for the woman who did not want him around.

But worrying about Daisy had unfortunately become second nature to Max, and he feared the trouble she could get herself into without him around to protect her from scoundrels and scandals. He only hoped her friends and servants watched out for her just as well as he'd tried to do.

Max yawned suddenly, and Abelton caught him at it.

His friend laughed. "*Your girl* has done irreparable damage to your ability to keep up with me," Abelton teased. "No stamina anymore."

Max shook his head, forcing himself to alertness by sheer stubborn will. "You'll be keeping up with me tonight, I'm sure."

"Where we're going, I wouldn't be so sure about that," Abelton said, eyes alight with mischief. All he would tell Max as they climbed into the carriage was that it was a long-overdue treat.

"Close your eyes now," Abelton demanded of him.

Max raised a brow. "Why would I do that around *anyone?*"

"I want this to be a surprise for you, of course," Abelton promised. "Trust me. All will be revealed in due course."

Max reluctantly closed his eyes and hoped for the best.

Abelton banged on the walls of the carriage to signal the driver, and they made a hard turn and then several more, until Max was thoroughly lost, but he suspected they were not headed for any of their usual drinking haunts.

The carriage stopped abruptly and lurched as the groomsmen jumped down to open the door for them.

"Open your eyes, my friend, and behold the wonder in store for us tonight."

He did, and raised a brow as he recognized the establishment. "Madam Bradshaw's?"

Abelton appeared crestfallen. "You've been here before? I thought you'd given up chasing skirts during the guardianship?"

"I received an invitation at the start of the season but was too busy to visit," he said carefully, lest Abelton tease him about the guardianship again.

"To think, I bribed a footman a hefty sum to gain admittance for both of us at short notice, and you had an invitation all this time. You had better pay me back for my lost funds," Abelton grumbled, brightening when Max agreed. "Let's go. The ladies are waiting."

Abelton bounded out onto the pavement, leaving Max to follow at a slower pace. He'd declined to visit this pleasure house for many reasons. Mostly because he'd thought it would be hypocritical to denounce sin to Miss Ellis while fornicating in such a place.

Since the end of the guardianship, though, he still hadn't lain with a woman. It was probably time. Time to shed the shackles of propriety entirely and be himself completely once more. Drinking, gambling, and debauchery were the staple occupations of any dissolute scoundrel, after all. Max had earned something of a reputation in his younger days—well before the guardianship and Daisy had come into his life.

He scowled for thinking of her again as he strode up the

stairs after his friend, announced himself to the majordomo, and they were admitted to the surprisingly elegant drawing room. He had to stop thinking of that blasted woman. He was better off without her, surely.

Inside, there wasn't proper attire to be seen on anyone. The women were in various states of undress, and the men making love to them did not seem to care about their clothing, either, or even that others watched what they did to their lovers.

Surprisingly, Max discovered he cared not to see such things anymore, and he looked around desperately for somewhere safer to rest his eyes. He spotted what appeared to be a dining room and headed there immediately, to see what he could find to satisfy his appetite.

He snatched up a plate to fill and studied an array of dishes that made his mouth water.

Abelton found him a few minutes later, when his plate was piled high, and his first words were to complain. "How can you eat at such a time? Look at the lovelies you're ignoring."

"You promised me food," Max complained back, as he finished filling his plate and headed for an out-of-the-way table to sit down. "I prefer a full stomach before debauchery." He took a bite of beef stew and savored the taste. "Almost as good as home," he noted in pleased surprise.

Abelton looked at him oddly. "Did you finally hire a decent cook and not tell me about it? Because I know for a fact your servants burn water and claim it is soup."

Max's face heated as he realized he'd misspoken. "*Her* home, I should have said."

Abelton laughed merrily at his mention of Miss Ellis,

something Max kept doing despite giving himself a stern talking to several times a day. She was not his, and that had not been his home. Daisy wanted nothing to do with him. But knowing he would never eat such wonderful fare again was almost an equal loss. Her cook's braised beef had melted in his mouth and must now be relegated to a mere memory. Something to dream about...as he often did Daisy, since kissing her.

On the nights he was cold sober, he cursed himself roundly for doing so.

"Ignore my nostalgia. I haven't eaten so well since then."

"I'll have to take your word for it, since I wasn't deemed refined enough to dine with you and *your girl*. Always afraid I'd sweep her off her feet, eh?"

Max sighed. "You had more than enough chances to impress her and never tried."

"I could never live with myself if I came between you pair," Abelton promised, hand on his heart.

Max rolled his eyes and refrained from comment. For a rake, Abelton was ridiculously romantic. But he'd not been invited to dinner simply because Max did not want the stories of his previous misdeeds filling Daisy's ears. Abelton was sure to have told her everything. "I told you. It was not my home to invite you to."

"Well, you took charge, moved in as if it was. If you miss the cooking so much, you should have taken her kitchen staff with you when she kicked you out," Abelton suggested. "You did hire them and gave up your own servant, Gibbs, to serve as her butler, too, didn't you?"

"Gibbs would never have left her by the end, so I did not bother to ask," he said with a shrug. "Besides, she treats them far too well for them to be dissatisfied with their employment and consider leaving."

"You mean you paid them too well when you first employed them for her," Abelton noted.

"She considers them family now. One does not break up a family," he advised. "They are all she has."

"That tender heart of yours is showing again," he murmured, looking highly amused. "It's how I knew you liked her so much."

Max put down his knife and fork. "Abelton, I had a job to do, and I do all things well. I could not leave her unprotected and alone."

Abelton raised a brow. "The way you were left alone after your father died?"

"Father never chose a guardian for me because I could take care of myself, and I did it well," Max insisted. "It is different for young women."

"Yes, it is. She is old enough to look after herself now, I suppose. She made her desire to do so very clear, but I'm not sure she doesn't regret it now," Abelton murmured. "She glances over her shoulder to where you always used to stand at balls."

Max shoveled food into his mouth, ignoring the ridiculous observation. Daisy would never miss him.

Abelton eyed the ladies watching them from the doorway, and then grinned. "Which one of them do you want?"

"None," Max said immediately, pointing to his plate. "I'm eating."

"But after. Blonde, or does the brunette take your fancy?"

A vision of Daisy as he'd last seen her flashed before his eyes. Defiant, impassioned first, and then after the kiss, flushed and lovely, brunette locks falling across her soft left shoulder, flowers from her hair scattered about her feet, and lips well kissed.

By *him*.

He shouldn't have done it. That kiss had revealed what he'd never suspected before. But it *also* explained why he'd behaved the way he had around her all season. Strict, unhappy, and downright possessive.

He knew who he'd prefer to be with tonight but did not dare say so out loud to anyone. Abelton would only encourage him to visit Daisy before dawn.

"I don't know. It will be a surprise to both of us."

Abelton could hardly keep the amusement off his face. "The leggy blonde looks like she's ready for some fun."

"Yes, I suppose she will be for the right price," he drawled, pretending that the exchange of money for pleasure didn't bother him now.

Abelton grinned. "I'll treat her well for the time we spend together, never fear."

Max nodded, but inside, he winced. Had he ever been as cavalier about bedding strange women for money? Right now, Max was offended on the lady's behalf to be picked out like livestock.

But that was how things went in a brothel, and on the marriage mart, too. A man could have any woman he wanted if the price was right. But beyond these walls, there were rules and hoops a gentleman had to contend with to have what he wanted in marriage. "Go get her, Abelton. I'll wait around when you're finished, and we can leave together."

"Don't forget to get your own woman tonight," he murmured. "Perhaps the brunette will have a temper like Miss Ellis, and that will improve your mood."

Max sighed and rested his head on his fist as his friend rushed away to charm his chosen lady of the night. He easily remembered all the times he'd done the same, and yet couldn't now remember the faces of any of the women he'd taken to his bed.

After Abelton and the blonde disappeared together, the brunette headed toward him, swaying her hips as she neared. "Good evening, sir."

He stood and bowed when she reached the table, but then realized he didn't have to act like he was at a society event. Still, Max gestured to the seat opposite him. "Would you care to join me?"

The lady nodded and sat demurely.

Max smiled at her, trying to like her more. "Would you care for tea or something to eat, perhaps?"

"Well, aren't you a real gentleman," she murmured, smiling in turn as she toyed with her hair. "I bet the society ladies lap up your attention like cats."

"I wouldn't know," he murmured. He was allergic to cats.

The prostitute arched one carefully painted brow. "Married?"

"I'm not."

"You've got a family then? You've got that good son look in your eye. First time in a pleasure house?"

"No, and definitely not the second."

The woman regarded him severely, and then appeared to freeze. "Are you one of them?"

Max laughed, taking no offense at her meaning. "No, merely starving for excellent food."

"Ah, well, you've come to the right place. The dishes are refilled every hour. And when you're done eating your fill, there are all sorts of other pleasures to indulge in here. Take one to bed or take us all."

Max's discomfort increased. He just wanted one woman. The right one. "Is that so?"

"Indeed." The woman set her arms to rest on the table, leaning forward to show off her cleavage. "You can start with me if you want."

But his eyes were drawn to her brow as her wig shifted, revealing her natural color as a blonde. Max did not want this woman, or any false brunette. While the view offered by a low-cut gown might have enticed him once, Max's first instinct was to tell her to cover up...just as he had done with Daisy Ellis by ordering the seamstress to raise her bodices higher if she wished to be paid.

The difference between the two women was striking, and if he was to view anyone's cleavage, he'd rather view Daisy's and kiss her witless again.

It was a realization that had come as a complete shock and unsettled him still a month later.

The woman across from him slipped the top button of her gown open, showing off a little more of her assets. He couldn't allow her to undo more, and again offered to fetch the woman a drink.

She declined.

"As you wish," he murmured and resumed eating, ignoring the lady entirely, while his mind struggled and argued that he couldn't possibly want Daisy Ellis more than any other woman. She was, had been, his ward for four years. He'd been responsible for her. Seduction should be the last thing on his mind when he thought of her.

She also hated him, and he'd almost felt the same.

But that was before the kiss. After...he was always thinking of kissing Daisy, though he tried so hard not to.

Yet thoughts of her, heated dreams, made him long to seek out what was once forbidden.

He ate, even though he found the food no longer appealing—but one thing was certain. He shouldn't be here, not if he had such thoughts about Daisy. She was meant for marriage, though. She was not a woman he could seduce and toss aside later. Her friendships in society could not be jeopardized by his infatuation.

But it still hadn't.

Eventually, he set the knife and fork aside and gestured to the servant to take his unfinished plate away. He patted his lips with the napkin. Knowing his only recourse was more of the usual. "What's your name?"

"Rose."

A flower. Just like Daisy. *Damn*.

He offered his given name and withheld mention of his title.

"It's a pleasure, sir," she murmured, smiling at him as if she found him the most captivating man she'd ever met. But it was dishonest, her smile. She wanted his coin, not him.

He should have sent her away immediately. He wouldn't —couldn't—spend a night in a prostitute's bed when he didn't care for her.

He cared about someone else more.

He stood and helped the woman up from her chair.

They strolled out of the dining area, into the larger drawing room together, where others were gathered around. The woman moved closer with every step until her breast was pressed harder against his arm. It was meant to be seductive; once, he might have enjoyed it and taken advantage of her interest.

But tonight, such behavior left him cold.

He asked for her hand, and then put money in her palm before he raised her hand to his lips and kissed the air above it. "Thank you for your company, but you should find someone else to share the night with."

"Are you sure I couldn't tempt you?"

"Not tonight," he answered gently, not wishing to give offense or explain. Not tomorrow, either. He would never come back here.

He gestured for a servant to ask him to fetch a drink while he waited for Abelton. There was somewhere he'd rather be tonight—and any other night of the week, for that matter—but he could not be there. He wasn't welcome. Not that he ever had been.

Max settled into a chair and told the waiter to keep his glass full.

Abelton had been right all along. It wasn't just the food he craved.

It was the maddening Daisy Ellis he wanted back in his life most of all. He thought of her all the time. Worried about how she got on without him. Wondered who she argued with instead of him, how many swains she'd been hiding under the linen-covered table—if she even bothered now—and who she was flashing her ankles at for the fun of shocking them.

Max eventually moved to a seat at a table where Hazard

was being played, and asked for a bottle to be left by his side when the footman reappeared. Pity it couldn't be a barrel but he'd make do. Max could always depend upon cards and drink to provide a distraction and forget the taste of his former ward's lips for yet another night.

Chapter Five

DAISY TOSSED a grape into the air and caught it between her teeth. She beamed and ate it with relish. "That's three for three."

"As ever, Miss Ellis, you are a wonder," said Gibbs, her butler, smiling as he absently polished a nearby table lamp.

"Thank you, Gibbs," she said, pushing the bowl of fruit toward him. "Your turn."

The butler held up one hand as he declined. "I'm afraid I must continue with my duties about the house, Miss Ellis. Perhaps I might send one of the younger maids to have a turn instead, or perhaps you might hire that companion you once talked about."

"A companion would try to tell me what to do," she reminded him, crossing her arms over her chest.

"They might also amuse you more than your gentleman callers seem to do lately," he suggested gently, clearly hoping she'd change her mind.

Daisy sighed. Yes, she might always yearn for company but was pleased that the worst of her gentleman callers had stopped coming around. They were only after one thing, and it was not the thing that Daisy wanted to give to just anyone. "That's all right, Gibbs. I just thought since you were here…"

She sent him away with a flick of her fingers, slightly embarrassed by her request now. Of course, a man in his prime was beyond parlor games now. Throsby, a decade younger at least, probably never played a silly game in his life, either.

It was not Gibbs's fault that she was dreadfully bored. Her married friend Gabby had been spirited away from Town for an adventure by her husband. It was the third time since the marriage and felt like an omen of what was to come.

Daisy had to learn to amuse herself again.

Her once-upon-a-time friend Justine still kept a distance. She had given up trying to mend fences with that girl, or trying to find out what was going on in her life.

Daisy hadn't met anyone else she could call on or go visit without a prior invitation being issued, either. She so missed the way things had been at the start of the season, without even Throsby's stomping about the house and perpetual bad moods to look forward to.

He had still not shown his face in society, but he was on her mind constantly. He had absented himself from every proper event for the last two months now, and she'd heard nary a whisper of what he was doing elsewhere.

She was near to the point of asking Abelton where he'd gone, and that was lowering.

Daisy snatched up another grape and rolled it between her fingers, growing angry with Throsby, and not for the first time. He had utterly lost his temper the last time they were together, and so had she, saying things they had both bottled up for years, it seemed.

Then he'd had the nerve to kiss her, and to her astonishment, it had been a rather unforgettable kiss, too.

That man had the gall to snatch victory away from her

on the eve of her triumph—the night she'd evicted him from her life. Nothing had been the same since.

She'd never have thought Throsby had it in him to be so passionate until that last night in his company. Had he been anyone else, she might have immediately sought a repeat performance of the kiss.

But of course, Throsby never would come around.

She'd made it clear his company was unwanted, and she was beginning to regret that. She *actually* missed him!

Daisy pressed her fingers to her temple and rubbed. She must have gone mad some time ago and not realized it.

But Throsby was gone off to live whatever life he'd had before the guardianship had begun, and that was probably good for him. They had not grown closer throughout the years they were forced together. He'd kept to himself, and Daisy had minded her own business, too.

She'd always thought they were quite opposites in nature. Throsby had been as predictable as mud. Daisy had loved nothing more than to shock him every chance she could. It had been a game, her little rebellions. Though there had been no escape from the guardianship for either one of them.

Throsby seldom talked about himself or any sacrifices he'd made when the guardianship had begun, until that last night here. She'd been a silly angry child to never learn what he'd had to give up, to move in with her. Beyond refusing to invite his friends to dinner, he'd said nothing of note about other friends or family members. Not a whisper of scandal or misdeed about him had reached her ears, and of course, nothing had suggested he was the kind of man to steal kisses like that.

She burst to her feet, annoyed with herself for obsessing about what Throsby might be doing with his days and nights. She ought to be glad he was gone from her life. No one told her what to do anymore. There was no one scowling at any young men who flirted with her, either.

Throsby had been beastly, far worse than any of the fathers of other young ladies enjoying the season, and far more present at her side. He was not friendly to anyone, really, especially not her. Not until the last minute. When upset, she'd never cried on his shoulder or sought comfort from him, not that he'd offered any.

But he *had* protected her from those devilish fiends of society who many called gentlemen. Those unfeeling scoundrels were determined to seek pleasure with no thought of the consequences for a lady.

She drifted through the house, as she had done for weeks, and eventually found herself in her father's old bedchamber upstairs…and the bed Throsby used to sleep in. The town house had been restored to its former configuration on her birthday, and the study was put to rights downstairs, too. But there was nothing of interest to her in either room, other than more reminders that Throsby had once been there.

She returned to her bedchamber and pulled the bell, sick of her preoccupation with Throsby. Her lady's maid was prompt in appearing and eager to be of assistance.

"Sarah, I think I shall go out after all today," she announced.

"To where, miss?" Sarah asked, rushing to the wardrobe and throwing the doors wide. Daisy had an impressive array of gowns now. She had her favorites, but any that Throsby had deemed appropriate were, of course, now barely worn.

"I don't exactly know where I'll go. Where would *you* go?"

The maid clucked her tongue. "You've got itchy feet again."

She glanced down. "Do I?"

"You're as restless as a cat lately."

Daisy sighed. "I haven't had a cat in a long time."

"Lord Throsby was allergic," the maid reminded her.

"Yes," she answered, remembering the horrible state of her new guardian's face and his endless sneezing when she'd once let a stray cat into the house without knowing he couldn't bear the animals.

He hadn't asked, but she'd quickly gotten rid of the creature for the sake of his health and improved mood, not that it had helped much. Thankfully, a neighbor had taken the animal, and Daisy had never dared visit it or let it into the town house, lest she make Throsby suffer so much again. "Perhaps I could get a cat now. There would be no danger to anyone."

The maid stilled. "What if Lord Throsby should call on you?"

She sighed. "I can't imagine that he will."

"But he could," the maid said, turning, eyes alight with barely suppressed hope. "His lordship might discover he left something behind."

Daisy sighed. The servants had grown fond of Lord Throsby, despite his growls and stomping about the house. "I was very thorough to send back anything that did not belong here promptly."

"Yes, I suppose you were," the maid murmured, a note of disapproval in her tone before she offered Daisy a gown in a soft shade of blue to change into. It was a gown that Throsby had approved of her wearing. Higher at the neck than fashionable, and therefore, far too modest to attract leers from scoundrels.

Daisy accepted the gown, letting the matter of acquiring a cat drop, too, as she readied herself for an outing to parts unknown. "Ask Gibbs to hail a hack and then fetch your bonnet."

"Yes, miss."

Perhaps a visit to the shops, or even the treat of an ice at Gunter's might lift her spirits. She had to do something to relieve the boredom of her own company. There was only so much pacing she could bear.

In Bond Street, she stopped first to look in Cabot's Haberdashery windows, where she'd shopped many times before. There was nothing much of note to see that was new or appealed to her greatly. Out of habit, she entered and purchased some ribbons and another pair of silk stockings for her collection.

When they stepped back outside, they fell in behind a pair of toffs who were deep in conversation as they strolled along.

"Did you hear about Throsby's luck last night?" one said.

Sarah gasped to hear someone speaking of her former employer, and Daisy quickly warned the maid to remain silent as they followed the men along the street.

"Gentlemen everywhere should know better than to gamble with him," the other replied. "He's always had the devil's luck, even so deep in his cups."

"I learned my lesson long ago never to trust him with my money," the first man noted.

"The viscount's luck took a decided turn for the better in other matters, too, hypocritical prig. Imagine the odds of him claiming a night with London's most particular courtesan, as well?"

"How do you think the Duke of Norrington will take it, sharing his mistress with his cousin?"

"Probably not well, when he hears of it. Someone will tell him eventually. I don't imagine Throsby can keep it quiet." The first speaker laughed softly. "This is the consequence of abstinence from the real pleasures in life for a gentleman," the other laughed. "Throsby's winning now, but I'm sure he'll not last long at this rate."

"And we'll be there to cheer his downfall, and recover our losses at the card table, too."

The pair chortled with glee.

"A man's character never really changes. Once a scoundrel, always a scoundrel, I say."

The pair flagged down a hack, climbed inside, and off they sped together.

Daisy stopped in her tracks, staring after the carriage in shock. "Is there another Lord Throsby in London?"

"They couldn't possibly be speaking of *your* Throsby."

"He's not mine." Daisy worried her lip.

"I do hope Lord Throsby is all right," the maid whispered, sounding frightened. "I think it strange he's not called on you."

Daisy and Throsby had not gotten along, so it was no surprise he hadn't called on her again. He would seek to avoid her, especially after their last conversation.

But after what she'd just heard, she was stunned. Throsby was not a scoundrel! He did not gamble or drink to excess. He had no interest in women, or courtesans. He was dull and predictable. A gentleman when it came to women. "I'm sure they were speaking of some other Throsby," Daisy assured. "Come on, I think we deserve an ice each from Gunter's before we head home."

Daisy turned back the way they'd come, heading for a spot to hail a hack—only to come face to face with *her* Throsby bursting out of a side street.

At least, the fellow seemed *similar* to her Throsby at first glance. A second, much longer glance was required to confirm his identity.

She hadn't seen Throsby since he'd surprised her with a kiss...and he was not the same man at all. His hair had grown shabby, his jaw was covered in horribly long stubble, and his attire was so rumpled, he looked to be wearing last week's clothes.

He looked like a pirate, a scoundrel, not a man who warned against scandal and vice.

His bloodshot eyes widened as he recognized her.

Daisy gasped, "Throsby?"

"Miss Ellis," he answered, his gaze shifting around nervously, but then he smiled for her maid. "Miss Finch."

Annoyed by the warmth of his greeting for the maid, Daisy stepped in front of the young woman. Then she glanced pointedly down the lane behind him. Yet she saw nothing to suggest where he'd come from or what he'd been doing down there. They were quite a distance from the usual gentlemen's clubs a man of his position in society might be expected to patronize.

She smiled tightly. "What are you doing here?"

"I'm going, I'm going," he muttered, misunderstanding the intent behind her question before hurrying away, lurching badly down the street.

Daisy followed a few steps behind for a short distance, startled by his abrupt manner, but his longer legs soon outpaced hers. She would not run just to keep up to talk to the man. Finally, he flagged down a carriage and disappeared inside.

"Well!" she huffed, as the carriage vanished round a corner.

"I barely recognized him, Miss Ellis. Lord Throsby seems ill."

Daisy set her hands on her hips and scowled. "Not ill. He is cup-shot, Miss Finch, but his manners are the same as they ever were," Daisy complained.

The maid giggled. "He was very polite to acknowledge me."

"Yes, he reserves all his worst behavior for *me*."

"Begging your pardon, miss, but can you blame him?"

The maid had been the one to hear all her complaints about Throsby's behavior over the season. They had become each other's confidants in a way.

"No. Not really," Daisy admitted honestly, as she glanced down the alley Throsby had emerged from again. "What was he doing down there, do you think?"

The maid confessed not to know but curiosity got the better of Daisy. She walked down the alley a little way. A few yards along, she saw a plain wooden door with a rose carved into the surface. They heard ribald laughter from the occupants inside. Women and men. Many of them.

The maid grabbed her arm and tugged hard to pull her away. "Such places are not for us to visit, miss."

"No, of course...and not for him once, I would have thought, too," she murmured darkly.

Daisy hurried back to the safety of Bond Street with a horrible feeling churning in her stomach. She was certain the rose signified a dwelling where a gentleman might pay for pleasure.

Hadn't those fellows just claimed Throsby had taken a mistress from a duke last night?

She was appalled. Had her argument with Throsby dared him to prove her wrong about everything and made him reckless?

For as long as she'd known him, Throsby had never kept a mistress or taken a lover. He'd drank sparingly and only occasionally gambled.

They climbed into a rented carriage, her nose wrinkling with distaste at the shabbiness, and she told the driver to take them straight home, forgetting to make a detour for the ices she'd promised her lady's maid until it was far too late to turn back. She apologized when she realized her oversight, but the maid didn't seem to mind; she was too busy chattering on about Throsby's ill condition.

Daisy listened with half an ear. Her shopping trip had been a waste of time and energy. The outing had left her feeling disappointed in her former guardian now, too. Getting drunk and gambling for a mistress' favor was not the way a gentleman, *her Throsby*, should behave.

But at her home, she found a huge surprise awaiting her in her drawing room.

Throsby was curled up on her settee, her servants

standing about watching him as he snored, making them all snicker.

She rushed to the front and shushed them. "What is he doing here?"

The butler stepped forward. "I'm afraid I don't know, miss. He let himself in with his key, lay down, and fell straight to sleep. I can't seem to wake him, either."

Daisy edged closer to the viscount, and in the close confines of the drawing room, she could detect the strong smell of spirits pouring off him in cloying waves. She'd seen the signs but missed the scent during their earlier encounter on Bond Street. She held her breath as she leaned over him and shook him by the shoulder. "Throsby, you can't be here."

Throsby caught her hand, brought it to his lips to kiss, and then clutched it tightly against his cheek. When he began to snore once more, Daisy recovered her hand with some difficulty and shuffled back to stand with her servants.

She looked at Throsby's lanky frame on the too-small settee, and then considered the strength of the servants at hand. None were young enough, or spry enough, to evict a man of his size without difficulty, even as a group. "I guess we just leave him there?"

"Nothing else to do with him," Gibbs agreed readily. "I suppose the sad news brought this on."

"What news?"

"I was talking with his valet yesterday and learned his cousin was thrown from his horse."

She hadn't known Throsby had a cousin, or any family at all. She'd never asked, and he'd never mentioned them. "How does that explain Throsby invading my home?"

"Well, he's no family to turn to for sympathy."

"He has his friends," she pointed out. "Abelton and... well, there must be others."

Gibbs sighed. "Yes, there are others. The cousin died a few days ago, leaving a widow and children. Did you truly not know about his family?"

"No. I haven't heard anything about them. I haven't even heard about *him* for weeks. We haven't spoken since he left."

"You spoke with him on Bond Street just this morning," Sarah piped up.

All the servants swiveled around and stared at her, brows raised.

"I'd hardly call that a conversation," she complained.

"Well, you kicked him out, so of course, he wouldn't drop by for tea," the butler threw out, and then winced. "A death in the family would upset him, and it is nothing he'd want gossiped about by us servants."

The other servants took the hint and filed from the room.

Gibbs nodded when they were gone. "I'm surprised he might care at all after the way that lot carried on after his father died."

"What do you mean, 'the way *that* lot carried on'?"

The butler looked at her with a sad expression. "His father died when he was little more than a dozen years old."

"Yes," she said impatiently, though she hadn't known his exact age. So young to lose a parent, much younger than she'd been.

"I was a footman in the household at that time, so this is not unfounded gossip. In short, the maternal side of the family attempted to take charge of him and came to drag him off to the countryside. He refused to leave his town house, but they forced him to go."

Daisy gasped. "They did not!"

"They did. Several times, in fact." Gibbs' eyes gleamed with amusement briefly. "The master ran back to the London town house each time, and then finally hid himself in the house so well they couldn't get him out again. I suspect he went out on the roof. So dangerous, but he was determined to remain in the only home he knew. Eventually, they gave up, but only after receiving assurances that they would be sent for if trouble arose."

Daisy considered Gibbs for a long moment. "You never sent for them, did you?"

"They were mean to him. He was just a little lad, but Lord Throsby was fearless, determined to take care of himself."

She nodded slowly, and then glanced at Throsby. "But this isn't that man. Look at him."

"No, this is what he came to be later—after several years of dissipation had taken its toll. Drunkenness and disorderly conduct were once commonplace events in his early life. I am sad to see him return to this sorry state."

"What changed him?"

"Why, *you*, Miss Ellis. Then and now. If I may be so bold and perhaps a little indelicate, the death of your father gave Lord Throsby the challenge he formerly lacked. He thrives in difficult situations."

Yes, she had challenged him at every turn, or at least tried to be as difficult as possible. She wet her lips and turned to Gibbs, a man who'd seen Throsby at his best and worst. Perhaps the only one who knew him truly. "Tell me, if he was so attached to his London town house, why did he insist on moving in with me here? Why not keep me there instead? Was I not good enough to live at that esteemed address?"

Gibbs reached out and touched her shoulder lightly. "If he had, wouldn't he have been as unfeeling as his distant relations? Your memories of your father were *here*."

She gulped, overcome by a wave of emotion and unwelcome tears. She probably would have run away, too, had someone tried to move her into their home after her papa died.

Throsby had done her the only service he could at that time. He wasn't the cruel monster she'd accused him of being.

He'd tried to make her loss easier to bear.

She let out a shuddering breath. "Better take the knocker off the door so no one finds him here," she whispered to Gibbs. "He'll need strong coffee when he finally wakes, and a hearty meal before we send him on his way again. Ask Cook to prepare his favorite dishes. Oh, and send for his valet, too. I should like a word with him."

Daisy dismissed the butler, and then shut the door behind him. She drew the curtains to darken the drawing room, and then moved closer to the sleeping man and watched him for a while.

Throsby, in his drunken condition, must have forgotten where he lived and brought himself home to the wrong house. She would have never believed those men on the street spoke the truth about him unless she'd witnessed him like this with her own eyes.

Drunkenness? And a mistress?

That wasn't the Throsby she recognized.

That wasn't *her* Throsby at all.

She fetched a blanket from a nearby box and, after a moment, draped it over his body, smoothing it along his broad shoulders and causing him to mumble her name.

"This will not do, Throsby," she said gently, and Daisy smiled as she brushed her hand over his hair in a halfhearted attempt to bring it to order. But Throsby's hair, like the man himself, refused to conform to her wishes of how it should behave or look.

She slipped from the sitting room and closed the door on her unlikely champion, impatient for the arrival of Lord Throsby's valet.

Chapter Six

MAX WAS EITHER HAVING a lovely dream or he was in Hell. He was back in Miss Ellis' wallpapered sitting room, watching her come down from the upper floor to either annoy him or meet a suitor. Across from him, the mantel-clock hands moved with agonizing slowness. He squinted, trying to focus on what she was wearing today in an effort to outrage him yet again.

Gods, it was agony to dream about being in this house. Back where he wished he could return. But he could not. There was no way back for him.

He turned his head and groaned as pain shot through his skull from the slight movement. He squinted again, quickly discovering he was not dreaming after all. He'd recognize that horrible flowery wallpaper anywhere. The velvet pillow cradling his cheek usually rested on another chair, though.

He was covered in a soft, fragrant blanket, and the room was cast in darkness. He was definitely under Miss Ellis' roof again but had no idea how he'd gotten here or when. The last thing he remembered was stepping through an unfamiliar doorway with Abelton at his side.

Max raised his head cautiously and looked around—straight into the eyes of his former ward. Miss Daisy Ellis.

The thorn who had once been firmly lodged in his side

for years, and the woman he couldn't seem to forget no matter how much he drank.

It was no surprise that she looked as pretty as she'd ever been, or that the scowl on her face conveyed the usual hostility toward him. She wore a gown of soft blue that made her seem ethereal in the near darkness.

He sat up very slowly, clutching his head.

"I see you've finally roused from your stupor," she complained, but only in a whisper.

Max appreciated her restraint not to yell at him. He probably deserved a good shouting-at for this breach of etiquette. "How did I get here?"

"You brought yourself and flopped down there, where you've snored for the last five hours or so."

"I'm surprised you didn't have me thrown out," he admitted.

She smiled slightly. "I considered it, but feared for my servants' poor backs, should they try to lift you."

"I apologize for the inconvenience," he said, wincing as he shook his head. "Why the devil did I bring myself here?"

He glanced across at Daisy Ellis and knew why, of course...longing.

Daisy sighed. "I suppose it was better than sleeping in a ditch, where you might have had your throat cut for that new ring you're sporting."

He glanced down at his hands and recalled why he'd drunk so heavily last night. There was no sense hiding the truth. "My cousin died, and his father sent it to me."

"Yes, I heard about your cousin only today. I'm sorry. Were you close?"

"Not particularly. The ring was stolen *from me* by him, another torment for not doing as I was told."

She frowned. "I thought you must have been close, since you were so disguised when we met on Bond Street."

He blinked at her. "We met on Bond Street? Today?"

"Yes, earlier in the day. Don't you remember speaking to me?"

He shook his head slowly, appalled by this, and rubbed a hand over his mouth, discovering he'd grown a beard somehow. "I appear to have lost track of a few hours."

"Several days, I should think, judging by that horrendous stubble on your face. Drinking too much will do that to a man. My father forgot his appearance when he drank heavily."

He winced at the comparison to her father. A drunkard and womanizer who few had missed besides his daughter. He glanced down at himself, and knew she was offended by his rumpled state, too. "My cousin dying was not why I was drinking."

"Did someone else die, then?"

"Not exactly."

Her eyes narrowed. "What is that supposed to mean?"

"I'm next," he confessed.

Her eyes widened in shock. "You're dying?"

"No. Unfortunately not." He sighed. "My cousin died and left a widow and two daughters to care for." He took off the ring, annoyed with what its return symbolized. It, more than anything, heralded the loss of his freedom yet again. He could not escape his fate. He could not fool himself into believing that someone else could take his place as head of the family one day. "I've been drinking heavily since I heard the news."

She nodded slowly, clearly confused by his words. "I'm sure that seemed like a good idea at the time."

"Stop being agreeable," he said in disgust. "You don't understand. I don't want this."

"I can understand only what you've told me."

He growled and swung his feet off the chaise and onto the floor, while his head spun and his stomach lurched. He clutched the seat beneath him, fighting for control and irritated that he'd misplaced it in front of Daisy.

"My cousin was to inherit the dukedom. With him gone, I'm the last blood relative who can."

"More wealth, power, and prestige for you, then," she continued heartlessly. "Everything a young lord dreams about, I imagine. All the unmarried ladies of society fainting as you pass them by, since you dress like that these days."

Max put his hands on his hips. "What's wrong with the way I'm dressed?"

"You look like a pirate."

He shot to his feet, outraged, and the world spun horribly around him. But suddenly Daisy was under his arm, supporting him, as if she cared that he might fall.

"Move slowly at first," she advised. "You've had quite the night, and if you fall, I will have to leave you there."

So much for her caring about him. "I was mourning the loss of my freedom, brief as it was."

She clucked her tongue, guiding him away from the settee. She pushed him down into his favorite chair. "Come now, Throsby, a future duke will have all the freedom in the world."

"Not if he's saddled with his cousin's widow and becomes guardian to not one, but two little girls," he said, unable to keep the bitterness out of his voice.

Daisy, however, burst out laughing. "Oh, no. Not again, and double the trouble perhaps this time."

Max shot to his feet again and headed for the front door on unsteady feet. He'd get no comfort here. No sympathy. He wouldn't stay to hear that her pity lie with the widow and those blasted children.

Daisy chased him to the front door and grabbed his arm to halt him. "Throsby, where are you going?"

"Away from you," he said, trying to shake her off. "I'm sure you'd prefer that."

"Not today. You'd think more clearly and feel better if you ate something before you step outside."

His stomach growled alarmingly loud in response to the mere suggestion of food.

"Besides, out there are dozens of heartless husband-hunting spinsters looking for the highest title to marry. A lord who is ill-prepared for a determined pursuit risks immediate leg-shackling."

He paused, realizing she spoke the truth. "Christ, it only gets worse."

"I would also suggest a shave and a change into fresh clothing, as well, before you step outside."

"I have nothing to change into here," he said, glancing down at Miss Ellis and scowling. "Someone made damn sure of that."

She smiled briefly. "That same someone took the liberty of sending for your valet. He happily agreed to return discreetly with whatever you would require to become presentable again," she said, appearing all too pleased with herself. "Your good standing in society is more important than ever now. You must think of your reputation."

Max froze as reality dawned. "I've inadvertently compromised you by coming here, haven't I?"

Daisy pursed her lips a moment, but he'd wager she had already had time to consider the situation he'd put her in. "I have no intention of mentioning you being here, and my servants already promised to do the same. They are concerned about you. No one has to know about your visit unless you or your valet tell them."

"He wouldn't dare," he growled.

"Good," she said, glancing past him and nodding. "Now, go and eat something before you faint away from hunger, and then freshen yourself upstairs."

He shook his head. "I never go upstairs in this house."

"But you must today. The contents of your former bedroom, my father's old chambers, were returned to where they belonged on my birthday."

"Oh," he said slowly, and then sighed. "Couldn't wait even one day to erase the memory of me being here, could you?"

She put her hand on his back and gave him a not-so-subtle push toward the dining room. "I prefer that lower room as the study it once was while my father was alive."

He nodded. They had argued a lot about him moving a bed for himself into that downstairs room. He'd felt it more appropriate that they slept on separate floors, given he was a bachelor. Daisy had seen it as him exerting his authority and resented the change. Now everything was back to the way she expected, Daisy seemed to have mellowed. "Thank you for your kindness today," he said, and finished with, "Daisy."

While he'd been her guardian, he'd never allowed himself to call her by her given name, even in private. It was too familiar, too intimate. The distance and formality had made their situation easier to maintain somehow. But things were different now.

Daisy guided him toward her dining room as if he were an invalid, which he almost felt he was. She helped him to a chair but did not offer to join him for the meal. She crossed the hall and shut the doors to the drawing room quietly, and left him all alone at the table in another dimly lit room.

Gibbs and his valet entered from another doorway and quickly whipped all the covers away to reveal a feast on the table.

Max almost fell into a swoon. "God, I missed this."

He hadn't had a decent meal since Daisy had unceremoniously thrown him out on the night of her birthday.

The butler and his valet loitered, faces full of concern for his wretched state. They filled a plate high and poured coffee for him. "May I express our sorrow at the news of your cousin's passing, and our immense satisfaction at seeing you here once more," Gibbs whispered.

"Thank you," he murmured. "But it was a mistake on my part that must never be spoken of again."

"Of course not. Should there be anything you need from us in the future, rest assured you will always find good help here," Gibbs promised.

He glanced at the butler, a man he'd known all his life,

and scowled. "Are you scheming for a new position for yourself, now I'm to become a duke?"

"No. Never," the man protested, looking highly offended. "I could never leave Miss Ellis untended."

"Good, otherwise I would have to regret the high wages I put you on."

"Never fear, your grace. Miss Ellis will always be my first concern. I only meant that should you find difficulty with securing satisfactory staff deserving of working for a future duke, I would be only too happy to help interview likely candidates. 'Tis a tedious business. But only if Miss Ellis permits me to help you, of course."

"Hmm, well, there is no guarantee of that, but I appreciate the offer," Max murmured, and then continued eating. He'd not taken on new staff simply because he wasn't spending that much time at his town house.

He'd been out with his friends most nights, trying to resurrect his interest in his old life and old haunts, without much success. All he needed at home was somewhere to sleep, water to wash in and shave with, and clean clothes. Food, such as it was, could be found elsewhere.

Now, he was trying hard to avoid thinking of what a future as an heir presumptive would entail. It would not be the pleasant, quiet life he'd hoped for.

Max hadn't visited his mother's family in a decade. The duke and that side of the family were difficult people, but he would have to put in an appearance at the ducal estate soon. The duke was a sour and taciturn man. Disappointed with everyone and everything. Max would face an inquisition and hear demands that he marry and get himself an heir.

His mood threatened to sour further at the thought.

Eventually, the act of shoveling food into his mouth and sipping strong, sweet coffee defeated his depression. He was determined to enjoy the novelty of an exquisite meal prepared just for him and what remained of a day under this roof.

He would not think about his late cousin anymore, making a marriage, or the weeping widow and children waiting for him to take charge of them all until he had to. They were under the duke's roof and, therefore, well cared for at present.

Max could pretend he was still a carefree bachelor for a little while longer, and then face up to his responsibilities with a clearer head later.

Just like he had when he'd learned of Daisy.

He glanced behind him at the closed door to the drawing room and heard nothing beyond. Daisy had left him to recover in peace, and he appreciated being spared a lecture about his conduct, though he was curious what she was thinking about him. She hadn't seemed overly angry that he was here.

Well, when he was utterly sober, he would have to come back and offer up a proper apology for the trouble and inconvenience his drunken behavior would have caused her and the household.

He was sorry she had to see him like this. No doubt he'd thoroughly disgusted her.

His valet returned to the room and set the day's news sheet beside his elbow, a freshly ironed copy. Max stared at the pristine pages, and he couldn't help the smile he wore as he skimmed the headlines.

Daisy must not be too cross with him at all if she gave him the news sheet of her own free will.

Chapter Seven

It was only yesterday that Lord Throsby had snored on her settee and then slipped away without a word of goodbye, so Daisy was surprised to see him sitting in the square before the house early the next morning. He was alone and facing her town house, and it was the exact time of day she and her maid always went for a walk, so he had to know she'd see him.

He looked...well...*better*. More himself with the sun shining down on his bare head and his hat resting on his knee. He appeared to have taken her advice and shaved, and even styled his hair a little neater, too. He was not as shaggy as the last time she'd seen him, and not so drunk that he could have mistaken his location. He must have recovered his composure after the loss of his cousin and the unpleasant news of becoming a guardian again.

However, that didn't explain why he was sitting in her square.

Daisy raised her parasol above her head to keep off the sun and descended her front steps with her maid following close behind, undecided about approaching him.

Throsby stood and took the decision out of her hands as he walked toward her. He raised his hand in a wave as he crossed the street. "Good morning, Miss Ellis. Miss Finch."

"My lord," her maid replied, before backing away to give them some privacy.

"Lord Throsby," Daisy answered after a moment, her gaze lowering to where a black band on his upper arm ought to be seen. "I did not expect to see you out and about at this hour, or at all, given your mourning."

That, and the sore head he could have woken with that morning, though she thought it unfair to bring it up.

"My cousin and I were not on good terms, and I will not shut myself away because society declares I should mourn my previous tormenter. The dead are the ones to be shut away, not the living."

"I'm sure you'll always do as you see fit," she said, though she approved his decision not to mourn a horrible person. "It is difficult to mourn someone you love, and given what I learned yesterday, especially harder for someone you have good reason to despise."

"Ah, I gather Gibbs told you all of my difficulties with my mother's side of the family," he murmured.

"They were mean to you," she said.

"Yes, they were. Indifferent, too. Cold and uncaring. They planned to move me to their country cottage and leave me there while they took up residence in my London town house."

"I can understand why you wouldn't want that and ran away from them," she began. "You were very brave to live alone at so young an age."

"Stubborn, not brave. A sympathetic neighbor stepped in and made enough of a fuss about them that they slunk back to the country in embarrassment and shame and never bothered me again. He checked on me from time to time," he admitted, and then sighed. "I suppose you thought I would remain drunk in celebration of my future elevation, but I'm not going to drink to excess anymore."

"I'm glad, because it doesn't suit you," she said, approving of his decision.

He leaned close and whispered, "I also haven't a cook like yours to make me feel so much better the next morning."

Daisy couldn't help but smile at that. "I could offer you the loan of mine."

"She won't leave you, and I'd think less of her if she did." He sighed. "You inspire exceptional loyalty in your staff, Miss Ellis."

"It's my happy disposition," she promised, flattered by his words. Her servants were her family. The only people she could count on, even though they were paid good wages to be there. Throsby hadn't liked her spoiling them the way she did, and they'd squabbled about that constantly. "Perhaps my staff could train yours."

"My stomach would know the difference," he promised, hand on his flat belly. "Miss Ellis, I wonder if I might join you and your maid on your walk today?"

Daisy considered refusing. She always had during the guardianship. But he'd lost his cousin and might need a sympathetic ear. They always argued, but she would try not to today. "It would be a pleasure."

"Thank you."

Throsby did not offer his arm, he never had, but he sighed again as he fell into step beside her. They walked silently for a while, leaving her square and beginning her usual trek around the next one. The maid followed but at an increasing distance the farther they went. Daisy waved at her to hurry up, but it was Throsby's scowl that brought her closer.

"How have you been?" he asked.

"I am always well," she promised, twirling her parasol to hide her agitation over the maid's silly behavior.

"And your friends? The Duke and Duchess of Mamble?"

"Well, I think. They're gone from Town for a while but are expected back soon. Had you not seen Mamble at your club to know?"

"Ah, no. I have not patronized the club or attended society amusements for some time. Not since...well, our last evening together."

She blushed, remembering their fiery exchange that night. And the kiss that followed. She blushed even harder as her eyes dipped to his lips. "Oh, I see. I suppose that is why I have not heard much of you *since...*"

"And you?" he asked quickly. "I assume you have been out in society a great deal...*since.*"

She looked up at him and noticed his scowl had finally returned. "Not really. I've been at home most nights, especially this week."

"Oh. I assumed you would have continued as you had been. You were always keen for a party."

"I am keen to meet with my friends anywhere," she told him. "Whether out or at home."

His scowl deepened. "You should be careful inviting your gentlemen into your home. No, forgive me—it is none of my business what you do anymore."

She forgave him for forgetting it was not his place to lecture her about propriety or her friendships. Not after his recent antics. Yet he had always been protective of her reputation. But according to the one piece of gossip she'd heard about him, and the state she'd found him in a few days ago, he'd tossed aside his good sense and was headed for ruin himself. She did not want that.

"Well, I imagine your mistress has kept you busy lately?"

He looked down at her in clear surprise at the impertinent remark. "Where did you hear I had one?"

Daisy scowled at him. "I saw you leave her residence yesterday, before you went home to the wrong house. Were you too drunk to remember her, too?"

His face paled. "You should not have seen me in such a state. Forgive me." He colored, and then shook his head. "As to the lady I left, it is not what you think."

"I heard you won Norrington's mistress in a game of cards," she murmured with an arched brow. "Isn't Norrington your maternal grandfather?"

She'd finally read Debrett's Peerage and learned a thing or two about Throsby's esteemed family tree.

"She'd become my cousin's mistress lately, and she was distraught at first." Throsby sighed. "She and Abelton hit it off, and I assume I left him sleeping in her bed."

"I see." She wet her lips. "But you have a lady of your own now, I trust?"

"I do not. I have not *since...*"

"Since?"

"A very long time," he admitted, and looked away.

Daisy frowned at him. She realized Throsby was embarrassed to talk about such things with her. As far as she knew, he had avoided all romantic entanglements during the guardianship. But that was long over, and surely, given his new and somewhat roguish appearance, he could attract the attention of at least one lady. Today he looked quite appealing.

They paused at a crossing, and before setting off again, she was shocked to feel Throsby's hand settled at the small of her back as he steered her across the street.

She found her breath once his hand fell away, as well as the awareness that his touch had not been unwanted. She cleared her throat. "When will you go to take up your duties as guardian to your cousin's children?"

"Not for some time, I hope. The children are too young to need husbands or get into much trouble yet. They have a mother, and the duke watching over them, so they do not exactly need me. The duke has grown fond of them, or so I'm led to believe."

"And the widow?"

Throsby pulled a face. "She is fine where she is."

"You are wise to leave them be in the place with good memories. She will be grieving for her husband for a long time, and would not like to be told what to do or where to go," she warned.

"If only that could be true," he muttered softly.

"I don't take your meaning?"

"She still wishes to become a duchess," Throsby murmured, inhaling sharply. He let it out slowly before he continued, "She's written to suggest I come immediately to marry her."

"*Marry her?*" Daisy looked at him in alarm, discovering his expression was one of disgust. "She offered herself in marriage to you while only just beginning her mourning period?"

Throsby nodded curtly, a brooding expression on his face now. No wonder he'd been drinking. He certainly had cause.

"How well do you know her?" She put up her hand. "No, don't answer that."

"I will answer you so you understand the awkwardness of the situation. We've met on three separate occasions. I don't find her at all appealing. There was never... I could not."

Daisy put her hand on his sleeve and squeezed, understanding what he could not eloquently or delicately put into words. "How awkward for you. No wonder you're not keen to take control of your wards' lives."

"It is a vastly different situation than I had with you," he hastened to say, covering her hand. "It is not as if they're alone in the world, the way you were left."

Daisy reluctantly pulled her fingers back from his under his grip, remembering how the life she'd known had disappeared in the blink of an eye with her father's death. Then Throsby had come and taken charge, filling it back up with something new and strange. He probably had done the best for her, but as a grieving girl, she'd resented his arrival and never let it go.

But she had to now. She'd taken stock of her situation and all that Throsby had accomplished in four short years. He'd increased her fortune by leaps and bounds and kept her in her own home with a household of capable staff she thought of as family. He'd left her with an abundance of love, instead of the emptiness that he must have experienced.

How odd to feel gratitude for him finally. She laughed at her reversal. "You might have to beat her off with a stick when you do meet, if she's already picking out her next husband."

"Laugh all you like, but it's not funny to me. She insists that she could provide me with a son in exchange for the title of duchess."

"Even when she didn't provide an heir for her late husband?" Daisy gaped, utterly astonished at what some women would do and say just to claim a title for themselves. "Although I suppose you must wait ten months to be sure."

"They were not sleeping together anymore. They've lived separately since the second girl was delivered. Even the duke knew that marriage was broken beyond repair, even for an heir."

Daisy walked on a few steps more. The thought of Throsby being married to such a woman was not appealing. It bothered her in unexpected ways. She was outraged and felt she ought do something to help Throsby avoid such a fate. But what could she do?

An affection-less marriage was to be avoided at all costs. Even future dukes ought to marry someone they could care about.

But the idea of him with another lady, someone he might enjoy kissing the way he had Daisy, did not sit right with her, either.

The possessive thought was so unexpectedly true that a hot blush immediately climbed her cheeks. She had enjoyed kissing him that one time. He *should* be kissing someone else like that...but she hated the idea.

Daisy glanced up at him, and her gaze was drawn to his lips. Throsby could try to kiss her again, and she would like to let him.

He suddenly put his hand under her elbow, peering down at her face. "Am I walking too fast?"

"No. Why would you imagine that?"

"Your face is turning red, and you appear to be breathing faster than normal," he murmured, his expression full of concern. "I should not like you to faint on the street."

If she fainted, would Throsby scoop her up in his arms and carry her home?

No matter how much she tried not to, Daisy blushed even harder at the thought. Her pulse sped up every time she thought of how Throsby had kissed her witless as soon as the guardianship had ended. She fanned her face with her free hand. "It is a little warmer than I expected it to be."

"Yes, we're having exceptionally warm weather of late." Throsby chuckled suddenly. "Do you realize this is the first long and entirely honest conversation we've ever had with each other?"

She gaped at him. "I have always spoken to you with great civility."

"Civility but not exactly patience. No, not at all."

She shook her head. "You were my bossy guardian and never let me forget it."

"Because I could not allow myself to forget my place, either. You were my responsibility, but you expected me to be like everyone else in your life. To become your friend. I could not have anyone assuming there was an intimate connection between us that might damage your reputation and end your chances of making a good match."

Daisy gaped, finally seeing their relationship from his side. Throsby had been concerned with appearances.

He'd been a stranger to her, a bachelor, and suddenly

made her guardian. Daisy had been a young woman approaching marriageable age then. If he'd been friendlier, would some small-minded fools have whispered about them and assumed they were to make a match, too, or worse... already intimate?

It was very likely someone would have started a rumor.

Daisy hadn't thought of him in that light herself. Not with the way he'd behaved toward her then. But he seemed different, now he was no longer her guardian.

She liked him because of that, too.

She liked him a lot more, and she hadn't the faintest idea what to do about that. A few more steps and they'd be back at her front door. Their time for conversation was again at an end. Soon, Throsby would leave her and go back to whatever he'd been doing these past weeks away from her, but she hoped with a lot less drunkenness in his days and nights.

One day, he'd take his leave of London, too, to pay his respects to the duke. Take up his duties as guardian, and perhaps marry his cousin's widow or someone just like her. Someone who wanted to be a duchess and might not care about the dreams of the man she married.

Daisy didn't know his dreams, either, but the thought that she might never see Throsby again filled her with incredible sadness.

He had a difficult future ahead of him. Throsby might not have been a man she wanted as a guardian, but he was the closest thing to a male friend she'd ever had. She couldn't treat him as if he was family, nor as a stranger anymore.

He was something else entirely.

They stopped at the base of her front steps, and the maid scrambled up to the door to knock.

Throsby removed his hat and bowed to her, causing his longer hair to fall across his eyes. He pushed it back with an impatient hand. "Well, Miss Ellis. This is goodbye again. I'll be on my way now. Again, my sincere apologies for any inconvenience I caused you and your staff during my last visit."

"Yes, it does seem to be time to part ways," she answered, regretting it must be so.

They had both suffered together through a guardianship neither had wanted. As a result of their disagreements, she knew very little about him and regretted that now. He had more family than she did, but he was still alone in the world.

"Would you care to join me for dinner tonight?" she blurted out suddenly.

Throsby's eyes widened.

"If you've no other plans, that is. I know you're probably very busy with your own life." She shrugged awkwardly, astonished with her desire to endure another private dinner with Throsby. It would be just the two of them, as it used to be, and hovering servants as chaperones.

A meal much like any other they'd shared before. Only now Throsby was not her guardian, and that made him more appealing company.

She shook her head. "Well...perhaps we could talk another time."

Throsby continued to regard her with obvious surprise at the unexpected invitation. She blushed and made no further comment, and that feeling of awkwardness grew as they stared at each other.

She wet her lips. "Cook fears that you're not eating

enough," she explained at last, wincing at how lame an excuse that was for such a scandalous invitation.

He put a hand on his belly. "She's probably right. I would love to join you for *any* dinner provided by your wonderful cook. What time should I arrive?"

She told him nine, two hours later than they'd usually dined together. Because at nine, many residents of the square would either be long gone off to their entertainments or just settling into their beds for the night. He might not be identified as coming or going from her home too easily.

"Nine it is. Until tonight, Miss Ellis," he murmured, returning his hat to his head and strolling off.

She watched him go for several long minutes and then rushed herself indoors. Once there, she leaned against the door and tried to catch her breath. She had invited a man to dine privately with her. How scandalous of her! How brazen. She'd never done it before with anyone, and certainly not with a gentleman who'd never wanted her to be scandalous in the first place.

Daisy jumped as a knock rattled the door behind her back, and she wrenched it open expecting to see Throsby only to discover her maid grinning at her.

"Oh, I am so sorry," she exclaimed in horror, stepping aside.

"Quite all right, Miss Ellis," the maid promised with a wide smile, walking in and shutting the door behind her. "A long stroll with a handsome viscount would overset any woman's good sense."

Daisy blushed. "Lord Throsby is coming to dinner tonight. Please inform Cook of that."

The maid giggled, and Daisy shooed her away.

Once alone, though, Daisy cursed her tongue. What a fool she was to invite Throsby to dinner. He was sure to have many other more important places to be now. And it wasn't as if he'd intended to see her again after their walk today. She'd surprised him, but he had accepted her invitation graciously, despite the impropriety of dining alone together.

She closed her eyes, reliving all the little touches they'd exchanged in so short a time today. Almost more than in the whole of their acquaintance, and not one had felt wrong.

And she foolishly hoped for more of that. Of a night spent blushing and anticipating how the evening would end between them. Her blush burned her cheeks. She would not mind if it was in kisses and soft sighs...and the hands of a handsome man touching her body.

The fact that she now thought of Throsby in those terms caused her to sit down on the stairs as her knees went weak with the shock.

Throsby, a man who had spent the whole of their acquaintance worried about propriety, had agreed to come and dine alone with an unmarried woman.

She started to laugh weakly and put her head in her hands.

Perhaps they had both gone mad.

Chapter Eight

"I'm not interested," Max warned, taking the tiniest sip of his tankard just to be sociable. He was determined to keep a clear head tonight rather than risk making a fool of himself again in front of Miss Ellis.

They were in their favorite tavern. Well, Max's former favorite. The loud, rustic establishment had lost its appeal some time ago.

"You need a woman in your life," Abelton assured him as he tossed back the contents of his tankard before he demanded another from the passing barkeep. "So do I."

Max hid a sigh at the repeated sentiment and the reason behind Abelton's insistence. Abelton's affair with his late cousin's mistress was over—ended almost before it had truly begun. Max's friend was melancholy about that today. He was staring into his cup and had sighed heavily all afternoon.

Max wasn't surprised and was glad it was over, too. Poor Abelton could never have afforded that particular woman for long. Giselle would have made him miserable in the end. What Abelton needed was a *good* woman in his life. Someone kind and thoughtful, not prone to theatrics to get her way. So far Abelton had been unlucky in love.

So had Max, but things were looking up for him now.

He'd refrained from confiding in Abelton about his

dinner plans for the night, determined to keep his unexpected invitation from Daisy a secret from his friend until he was more certain of what it signified. He did not want to assume anything with her. Besides, Abelton would only crow with laughter and claim Max had felt something for her all along, should he learn.

But Max surely hadn't until the kiss.

Everything had changed for him after that night.

He imagined he and Daisy were becoming friends of a sort, though. At least, that is what he hoped he'd accomplished by their morning walk together and confessions. He would like to return to society amusements, to the balls and the luncheons that had once so bored him, and not have to worry about his presence upsetting Daisy.

Max surveyed the taproom once more and found nothing and no one of interest to him here. He should have gone home hours ago, but Abelton's melancholy required company. But the longer he stayed, the more anxious he'd become about the dinner ahead.

Would they argue or end the night in another stolen kiss?

He hoped for the latter, but only after they'd had a chance to talk more beforehand. This morning's conversation had only whetted his appetite for more time with Daisy. With the guardianship out of the way, he'd enjoyed the stroll with her.

In fact, confiding in her had been a relief. Daisy understood his situation, even if she had been clearly amused by his becoming a guardian again. She had offered helpful advice on how to deal with his new responsibilities. Max had never expected his cousin to name him as guardian to his daughters, but it would be just like him to dump his responsibilities on someone he despised. He'd always been a selfish, uncaring prig. A bully. He'd stolen Max's father's ring—and anything else he could lay his hands on that Max valued—during the short time they had infested his London town house.

And his widow, Honoria, was the last woman Max would like to be in close quarters with for any period of time. He'd never marry such a grasping female. She was the complete opposite of Daisy, who was all sunshine and practicality. Possessed of a heart full of kindness toward others.

Honoria was spiteful and vain, eager for a title she'd never be entitled to now. He'd have to be especially careful around her when he saw her next.

"What are you looking so grim about now?" Abelton asked, startling Max out of his contemplation of the future troubles.

Max pushed his drink aside. "I was thinking of going home."

"Well, don't let me keep you if you want to spend another night all alone in that big empty house of yours," Abelton murmured, swiping his drink and sculling it down. He wiped his mouth on his sleeve. "I'll be here, drowning my sorrows on my own," he continued.

Max almost changed his mind about leaving, until he saw a handsome woman watching them closely. He quickly realized her interest was in Abelton, and not himself.

He hid a smile. Abelton was a popular devil who attracted ladies in spades everywhere he went. He just could never keep one around for long.

"I'm sure something will come along to distract you after

I'm gone," Max promised, as he pushed up from the table. "Will you be at the club later tonight?"

"No, worse luck. Atherton is hosting a soiree. Must attend, since we're related," Abelton grumbled. "You should be there, too. The last thing I want to do is be bored by proper ladies without you by my side. Who knows, perhaps your girl will be among the guests."

Max squeezed Abelton's shoulder. Daisy would be with him, at home. "She's not my girl."

Abelton slammed his tankard down. "Only because you won't stir yourself to claim her."

Max did not bother to argue and bid Abelton a good night before he made his way toward the woman, who was still watching Abelton. He slipped her a crown. "See if you can cheer him up."

The woman palmed the money and smiled brightly. "I already planned to once you were out of the way."

Abelton was in good hands then. Max lingered long enough to see the woman headed across the room but did not stay to see how her arrival was received. Abelton could manage his love life.

Max had his own to worry about.

Daisy was still very much on his mind. She had made his future seem not as bleak as it had at first, and all in the space of a short walk.

Out on the street, he strolled along the pavement, avoiding eye contact lest he see someone from society who just loved to stop and gossip. He did not want to be late reaching home. He had to ready himself for seeing Daisy again and make a good impression.

He was approaching a street corner nearest his home

when he heard a woman cry out in alarm. He rushed forward when he spotted Miss Justine Dawes reaching for something dropped on the dirty roadway.

"Watch out!" he shouted, as a carriage barreled toward her and her outstretched hand, cutting the corner dangerously close to where she stood.

He pulled her back in the nick of time, and the item she'd been reaching for was lost under the churning of a carriage wheel, forcing it into filth.

He righted her quickly and stepped back, catching a glimpse of her distraught face. "Miss Dawes, are you all right?"

She looked at him and then the book on the road, and a shuddering moan left her. "I was."

She turned away suddenly and ran from him.

Max was stunned by the haste of her departure. But she was a strange one, Miss Dawes. He'd never quite known what to make of her, or her friendship with Daisy. His previous ward and Miss Dawes were like chalk and cheese. The former was utterly open with her opinions, while the latter chose every word with more care.

That their friendship had ended the way it had did not surprise him. But he was certain the young woman was not happier for the loss of Daisy's company.

He glanced at the book lying in the muck and wrinkled his nose, then checked for traffic before he stooped to pick it up by the only corner free of filth.

It seemed familiar, and he vaguely recalled Miss Dawes always carrying a book with her when she had visited Daisy. Max thought it important enough to try to salvage.

He carried it between two fingers until he reached his town house and immediately called for his valet.

Max held the ruined book out toward the man. "See what you can do to clean this mess up, but a word of caution: do not read one word of what might be written inside. It is not mine, but I know the owner."

The valet scowled. "As if I have time to read anything these days, my lord."

"I'll hire more staff to help you soon, I promise," Max offered, hoping to placate the man.

The valet huffed and muttered, "That's what you said last month," as he carried the book away, held gingerly between two fingers the way Max had done. He disappeared down the servants' staircase, grumbling about being ill-paid for all the work he was expected to do.

Max winced. He *had* been neglecting his responsibilities here, few though they were. He just never seemed to get around to writing an advertisement for new servants. Perhaps he should accept the help of Miss Ellis's butler, who seemed keen to find competent staff for him. But he'd have to talk to Daisy about that. Get her permission first.

She'd probably like that.

When Max looked around, he noticed how empty the place was now. His footsteps echoed as he moved from room to room. It must be as lonely for the valet as it was for Max.

Daisy's servants had been underfoot so often in the smaller town house that Max now had trouble imagining an entirely new staff doing things for him. He'd become accustomed to living in the Ellis household, and the lively staff there now made his home feel foreign.

After his father died, Max had lived alone for years and

never bothered to replace servants as they left his employ. He'd simply closed up the rooms he had no use for and never thought about them again. But he would have to do something about the state of the house soon. The unused rooms would be stale and dusty.

He turned for his study, the only room he'd spent any real time in since his return, and threw himself into a well-worn leather armchair by the fire. His town house was far too large for a solitary bachelor, but he'd refused all offers to lease the place from friends with growing families when he'd gone to live at the Ellis abode.

He'd missed his home, missed having his own space, and yet he also yearned for the smaller, chatter-filled Ellis household and the happy staff. The tiny rooms, the squeaking floorboards above his head as Daisy moved about, and the daily fight with her over possession of the newspaper.

He was lonely here.

Max shook his head and moved to his desk, sorting through the correspondence he'd neglected to answer in the last month. He found two invitations for events he'd missed last week, another pair for future dates, and yet another letter from his cousin's widow that he tossed straight into the fireplace to burn without reading.

The other letters were all for business matters, and he set them aside for tomorrow. But he picked up the new invitations again, pondering which Daisy might have been invited to. He wanted to spend time with her, and not just in private.

He would have to find out where she'd be going during dinner tonight, if he could catch a moment alone with her.

The fastest way would be to ask her outright, but what if she didn't want to tell him in front of others? What if everyone at the dinner wondered why he asked? He groaned, frustrated with the way things were currently.

He had never been one to rush. Preferring to make considered choices in lasting matters, and he hadn't been one for impatience when it came to the women in his past.

But Daisy was different.

Tonight he would have a chance to discover if she could have any interest in becoming his friend. A good friend. But he did not anticipate an easy path to friendship with Daisy.

As for his interest, this was no idle fancy of his. For years he'd turned his back on his family and the idea of having his own. But now, there was a great appeal in sharing his days with someone...and he thought he would like it to be with Daisy Ellis.

Max wished to explore what might be possible between them. See if something beyond what they'd shared so far was possible without breaking too many rules, or being caught misbehaving together. Daisy was not a woman he could toy with the affections of without regard for the inevitable consequences of doing so. A marriage between them was possible if Daisy had any interest in him. He did not need to wed a great fortune, nor did he have any desire to curry favor with a match to a daughter from the oldest family in England.

But courting Daisy would still be a delicate undertaking. He was half afraid she'd laugh or throw him out again if she knew too soon the direction of his thoughts.

Though if she liked him enough, if they married, she could argue with him for the rest of his life if that made her happy, because then he'd always know where she was and who she was tormenting.

Max glanced at the mantel clock and swore. Half seven o'clock already? Where had the time gone? He rushed from the room and upstairs to his bedchamber, calling for his valet and determined to dress to impress if he could.

Chapter Nine

Throsby appeared in Daisy's front hall at precisely nine o'clock, looking exactly as Daisy had expected him to. Freshly shaved, dark evening coat and breeches. Gleaming white shirt and cravat. She peeked at him through the gap in the door from another room, and her heart clattered against her ribs.

Gibbs greeted him with obvious joy and took his coat and hat.

"Am I the first to arrive, Gibbs?" he asked.

Daisy winced. Oh, dear. Throsby had come expecting to be one of a handful of guests at a proper dinner tonight when it was anything but.

"Yes, my lord," Gibbs replied, knowing full well that no one else was expected.

The dining table was set for an intimate dinner for two, but the doors were shut and hiding that fact. Daisy wanted nothing to get in the way of an honest conversation with Throsby tonight. Other guests would only be in her way.

She took a deep breath and stepped out of the shadows so Throsby would see her waiting for him. She was wearing a silk gown in dark blue that now possessed a lower neckline than he'd ever allowed her to wear.

Throsby paused a moment to take in the view, and then

recovered his composure. He moved toward her and bowed. "Good evening, Miss Ellis."

Daisy dipped him a curtsey. "Lord Throsby. I am so glad to have you here tonight."

He nodded and glanced around. But there was no one else for him to talk to. "It was a pleasant night for the short journey here."

She laughed softly. "I'm glad for the sake of your coachman and the grooms," she murmured. "Would you care for a drink, my lord?"

"Nothing for me yet. I am happy to wait for the other gentlemen and wives to arrive."

Daisy caught his eye. "There are no other guests expected here tonight, my lord. Only you were invited."

Throsby froze. "None at all?"

"No. My invitation was solely for you."

Throsby scowled at her.

"That scowl does not work on me anymore," she warned him, and kept smiling.

"As if it ever did," he grumbled sourly.

Daisy held up her hands. "Now, you can scowl and leave with an empty belly, or you can stay and feast with me and ignore that it is improper. Cook has been slaving away all day just for you."

His cheeks colored slightly. "She shouldn't have gone to so much trouble."

"It was no trouble," she promised.

Thankfully, Gibbs arrived and announced dinner was ready, cutting off a conversation about impropriety that would never end.

"Shall we go in, or will you be proper and leave?"

Throsby seemed undecided for a moment but then nodded. They walked to the small round table side by side, and Throsby helped her into her chair. He sat down at the other place setting, right next to hers instead of opposite, as he'd always done before.

In the candlelight, the night turned the atmosphere between them romantic, and she smiled as Gibbs laid her napkin across her lap. "I'm starving."

Throsby snapped out his napkin as he always did and looked expectantly at her. "I am too."

Daisy fought a blush as the servants trouped in, carrying an array of mouthwatering dishes. Throsby seemed about to swoon as his favorite dishes were set around them.

He glanced her way. "I am truly being spoiled now. This is excessive."

Daisy laughed and dismissed the servants. She and Throsby could serve themselves.

She started eating and, between mouthfuls, asked Throsby about his day.

"Then she just turned and ran away," Throsby finished, ending his tale about an encounter with Miss Dawes and wincing. "Did I do the right thing, retrieving the book for her? I'm not certain now."

Daisy put her hand over Throsby's where it rested on the table between them. "You did well. Justine was always carrying that little book. Sometimes I caught her scribbling in it, lost in her thoughts. She never told me what she was writing in there, and she will want it back, I'm sure."

"It is being cleaned first, and then I will return it to her at one of the balls this week. Would she attend the Norris or Bexley amusements, do you think?"

"She would be attending both, but you should not return it to her there. It would look strange to receive a book when she is there to dance," Daisy advised, a teasing smile on her face as she waited for Throsby to reconsider his plan.

"Ah, yes, of course," he said. "I will return it to her at home at a later time then."

She fidgeted in her chair, frustrated by that decision of his, too. "Hopefully, her sister will not read more into your visit than she should. You are to become a duke, remember, and a young woman in want of a husband might assume you are calling for a completely different reason."

He pinched the bridge of his nose. "Yes, there are so many misunderstandings to guard against everywhere I want to go now," he complained.

"Justine is ambitious, so you must always be careful," she said, fighting with her certainty that Throsby had a large target painted on his back. Women everywhere would line up to catch his eye. Unmarried gentlemen destined for elevation to the rank of duke were scarce on the ground this season. Gabby had caught the last bachelor duke she knew of. "I suppose your poor valet had the job of cleaning Justine's journal, since his father was a bookseller?"

"Yes, and he wasn't happy about it at all. But there's only him I trust to give it to. There's a maid of all work who comes in each day," he answered, setting his napkin on the table and fussing with it.

She stared at him in surprise. She'd been inside Throsby's town house once, a brief visit of half an hour and no more, but knew his home must be twice as large as hers. "Why do you not have more servants by now?"

"My needs are small, but I must hire some soon before

my valet gives his notice due to overwork and loneliness. I wonder if you would permit Gibbs to assist me?"

"You want Gibbs back?"

"Not back," he said quickly. "He has vowed never to leave your employ. But he offered to conduct interviews for me. He claimed a future duke needs the right staff about him."

"He is not wrong about that," she said, considering the request. Gibbs had little to do here, now that Throsby had left the house. If Gibbs helped Throsby, the butler would only be polishing the silver once a day, instead of the three times she caught him at it lately.

Daisy probably had more staff than she needed anyway, but she couldn't bear the idea of letting anyone go just because they were without enough work to fill the hours.

"Gibbs and others may help you if they want to."

"Thank you. Gibbs has been a great help to me through the years, as has my valet."

"The servants remarked only this morning how much they miss your valet, by the way, but that might be on account of him always being the one to iron the paper."

Throsby met her gaze and ignored her mention of the paper as he continued. "Miss Dawes seemed unhappy."

"She is troubled indeed, but over what I cannot say. I've had a feeling she wished to speak with me for some time, but something always stops her. But it has to be Justine who makes the first move to resume our acquaintance. There was no need for subterfuge over her feelings about Lord Brookes, if she had liked the man as much as Gabby and I once thought she did."

"Now neither one has married him." Throsby shook his

head. "Though I don't imagine your friend was dissatisfied with becoming a duchess in the end."

"No, but the title is not why she married her duke." She wrung her hands, studying Throsby. "You do realize that, don't you?"

He nodded. "Love. An almost unheard-of state for most great men of the *ton* to admit to suffering. But Mamble admitted it freely to anyone who would listen. They chose with their hearts, not because of her dowry or his title."

Daisy wet her lips, suddenly nervous about the subject of marriage. Throsby had talked a great deal about her making a good match, but never had he given her a clue as to what he might want in a wife himself. "Is that what you will do, my lord? Will you choose love over a great and advantageous match?"

"I would prefer to, but I've yet to find myself in that position." Although he frowned the next moment, and his eyes dropped from hers. A flush of color spread over his features, and he reached for his glass suddenly to take a small sip of wine.

She studied his expression, and felt a blush forming on her cheeks at his discomfort. She wasn't sure what it meant, but the subject bothered him. Throsby had changed so much since the guardianship ended that she could no longer read his mood or gauge his reactions.

Flustered by that, she picked up a plate of sweet cakes to end the meal and offered him first choice.

Throsby groaned. "I want one, of course, but I couldn't possibly eat another bite."

Daisy set the platter of cakes down and laughed softly at him. Throsby had eaten very well tonight, stating he'd been starving for lack of a good cook at home. Cook would be so pleased to hear he enjoyed the meal, and Daisy was, too.

If Throsby had not employed enough servants yet, he must be eating at his club a great deal too often. "Just as well, or there'd be nothing but crumbs for any morning callers tomorrow. Cook has outdone herself."

"She has, and she always does." He leaned his elbow on the table, gazing at her directly. "Perhaps I could convince *you* to dismiss Cook, so she has no choice but to come and work for me instead?"

"Not a chance," she said quickly, eyes narrowing. But she was surprised to discover the viscount was merely teasing her. "Too much of this and you'd only grow fat, the way you eat."

"I managed to keep my trim figure while I was your guardian, despite all the endless dinners we were invited to this season," he protested, putting a hand over his flat belly protectively, making her laugh at his display of vanity.

Perhaps she'd drunk too much wine with dinner, but she felt utterly charmed by Throsby tonight.

Daisy gazed at him as if she'd never truly talked to him before. Dinner tonight had been vastly different from their previous meals together. They were at ease with each other for once. Teasing and being teased had never been so enjoyable before. "I always wondered how you did that. I assumed you boxed or did something equally vigorous while you were out."

He quirked a brow. "Chasing you around ballrooms kept me fit."

"You never *caught* me doing anything wrong," she protested.

"You were thinking about it, though." He sat back. "It was deterrent enough that you knew I was watching you and your admirers, so you all behaved yourselves."

"You speak of my admirers as if there were legions," she complained, flipping her hand around. "I don't see them around now because you scared most away."

He glanced to the floor and started to lift the tablecloth. "Are there no scoundrels hidden away under this table?"

She blushed at the reminder of her deceptions that hadn't gone unnoticed, after all. "I haven't done that since you left."

"I'm glad to hear it," he said, scowling once more. "Anyone worthy of your hand in marriage should have stood their ground and faced me like a man."

"And what would you have done with them then?"

"Agreed to the match if you'd said you wanted it," he claimed immediately

She blushed. "There was never anyone in particular I wanted."

"No?"

"No." She squirmed, thinking of him and that heated kiss they'd shared. "Shall we withdraw to the sitting room to continue our conversation?"

"Why not."

Daisy rose from the table, feeling awkward all of a sudden.

Perhaps there never had been a man worthy of her hand in marriage or brave enough to endure Throsby's scowls and seek his approval. But that also meant she was not worthy of fighting for. It was a lowering thought, indeed, and one that would require time to reflect upon in private.

She moved toward her favorite chair, where she'd spent much of her morning calls with Throsby looking stern and forbidding in his own nearby chair. It was unsettling how right it felt to have him back here again. But he would leave at the end of the evening and she'd be alone again.

She did not sit down straight away.

"Did I say something wrong?" Throsby asked suddenly.

"No. Not really." Daisy shivered and rubbed her arms, unable to find the right words at first to explain her sadness. "Men only choose women they find appealing, don't they?"

"Women often do, as well," he countered. "Those in our society marry for a variety of reasons though. Connections, wealth and land, and want of a title, particularly."

"I guess I failed on all counts then. No one chose me this season because I have and want none of those."

Throsby drew close, and his fingers settled on her shoulder. He turned her to face him. "I think you are very eligible for marriage."

She shivered at the husky tone of his voice and looked up into his eyes. "Then why did you never tell me that? I've spent the whole season doubting my appeal."

He frowned again. "What I think of you shouldn't have made a difference. You have to make your own decisions in this world, especially when it comes to choosing the man you would marry. I would never presume to do that for you, or for anyone."

"You were my guardian!"

"I'm not now." He reached out and caught her gently by the chin. "I have always thought you the most surprising debutant of the season, vexing and unpredictable perhaps, but lovely, and if no one but me saw the challenge in you, then the fools deserve to have missed their chance to be made happy."

Daisy gaped at Throsby, astonished that he could say something so romantic she might swoon.

He wasn't her guardian anymore. He was different, *they* were different, freer than they'd ever been with each other. She wanted more of the unexpected thrill his words filled her with, and more of his touch, as well.

"Thank you," she whispered as she reached for his face, too, lightly touching his clean-shaven jaw. His skin was warm and supple under her fingers. "But who are you, and what have you done with *my Throsby*?"

He laughed. "I'm here."

Daisy's heart fluttered at the sound...and she rose on her toes to claim his mouth in a soft kiss she'd been longing for all night.

It was different, being the one to kiss rather than wait. He was tall and she was short. But then it didn't seem to be a strange thing to do at all when he kissed her back.

Throsby was as exciting a kisser as she remembered, though she still wasn't prepared for the storm of arousal that flooded her senses. He was not a passionless man, and she had accepted that startling fact. Why else would she be dreaming of his lips against hers again, or had no other man interested her since their first kiss?

Throsby turned them, moving her with him, and her back landed against a papered wall. He leaned away only long enough to shut the door to the hall and lock it. Then his hands were cupping her face again, and his lips were setting her senses ablaze.

She held on to his coat but quickly decided it was in her

way. She shoved it back from his shoulders, and Throsby helpfully shrugged it off, letting it fall to the floor.

She put her hands on the sleeves of his upper arms, covered in fine white linen, and discovered him more muscled than she expected and blazing hot under her fingers.

She reached immediately for the buttons of his waistcoat.

Throsby suddenly covered her hands, stopping her assault on his clothing.

Daisy opened her eyes slowly and looked at him. Passion blazed in his eyes, but then that expression slowly dimmed. Their kisses ended, and Throsby sighed, pressing his head against hers. "This will not do, Miss Ellis," he warned.

Daisy would have staggered but for his arms closing about her and pulling her tight against him.

He caught up one hand and kissed her knuckles. "I must go."

She gaped at him. "Now?"

"Now. Before it's too late to stop."

Her eyes widened. She did not want him to leave. She wanted more of the feelings he stirred inside her. He'd fooled her into thinking he was a chaste man, but he could be so very wicked if given half a chance.

Something held him back. Something about *her*. About them being together and kissing. He was lovely and passionate, but passion always comes with a price.

She spread her hands over his heaving chest, realizing that despite his words, he was as affected by their kisses as she was.

It was remarkable, his restraint, though. She would have

gone along with anything he suggested just to keep him close, had he dared ask for more.

One of them was thinking about the future, and it hadn't been Daisy. But then, hadn't Throsby always cared about her reputation above all else? Some things about him hadn't changed one bit, and she was oddly relieved by that.

She patted his chest. "All right. You can go."

Throsby snorted a laugh. "Why, thank you, Miss Ellis."

Daisy caught his chin in her hand and drew him back down for another, softer kiss.

When their lips parted again, he said, "Can I call on you again? Or will you be attending a ball soon? I have a few invitations, but I will only accept if I know you will be there to enliven the evening."

Daisy tried not to show her excitement over his interest in attending the same balls again. He hated them. "You may indeed call on me here anytime, or speak with me at the Sanderson ball. Who knows...I might even allow you to kiss me there."

Throsby kissed her hard then, drew her arms up over her head, and held them pinned against the wall.

Then suddenly he was gone, and she opened her eyes to find him standing at the doorway with his coat clutched in his fist, shaking his head. "What have I said about encouraging scoundrels to take liberties?"

"You're hardly a scoundrel, Throsby," she assured him, leaning against the wall because her legs were trembling and her hands itched to drag him back.

He growled and took a menacing step in her direction, but that thrilled rather than frightened her.

"I must be doing something wrong if you think I'm not

one by now. Should I display my interest in seduction again?"

She gaped. He really would seduce her if given the chance. Daisy's lady parts quivered at the exciting thought of what might happen if she spent a night in his arms, in his old bed or hers. But then caution prodded her to behave, and she held out her hands to ward him off. "Better not rush our affair."

His brow rose high. "Our *affair*?"

"Indeed," she agreed, thrilled by that fact. "But you better go home now, my lord."

He nodded, and it was clear he approved of her decision to kick him out before things went too far.

He bowed deeply. "Until next we meet, Miss Ellis."

"Good night, Lord Throsby," she said. "Pleasant dreams."

"My dreams…" he began, and then his lips twitched. "They'll be of kissing you again."

Daisy blushed as he disappeared out the door then exited the town house. Then she slowly collapsed to the floor in her very first swoon over a romance she'd never seen coming, but planned to enjoy to the full.

Chapter Ten

Max smiled at the hostess. "Lady Sanderson. So good to see you again?"

The older lady fluttered her fan. "Lord Throsby, how delighted I am to see you at last. I was starting to think you'd forgotten me."

"Never. Apologies for my tardy response to your invitation," he murmured. He was late, but not unforgivably so. The ball was well underway, and his leaving home had been at the very last minute. He'd been torn about what to wear.

But as the hostess's eyes roved over him from head to toe, he concluded that he had made the right choice. She seemed impressed that he had chosen to wear one of his more flamboyant waistcoats, and his father's dress ring, too.

He hoped he didn't look like an overstuffed goose, and that Daisy didn't laugh if he did. "I have been much involved elsewhere, but I would never miss an event of yours."

"Family obligations can be so wearying. I was very sorry to hear about your cousin," she murmured solicitously. "So tragic to die so young."

"He will be missed," he said, but likely only by his children and mistress.

"Well." The hostess' eyes brightened suddenly as she

dismissed his dead cousin from her mind. "Let's see which young ladies you don't know yet?"

Max groaned under his breath. He knew everyone in society and their daughters, too. He'd extensively researched potential friendships to strike up and rivalries to avoid before launching Daisy upon society. But it had been done in the interests of helping her to make a suitable match. Now his interest in Daisy's future had changed to something rather selfish. He did not want her to marry anyone but *him*. Not after their second romantic encounter.

He saw Daisy across the room. So did Lady Sanderson, and he sensed she deliberately turned him in the opposite direction. Lady Sanderson showed him off like some highly prized stallion, stopping often to speak with matrons who all had daughters with large dowries to marry off this season. He couldn't seem to shake her clutches, either.

He was forced to re-meet all of the unmarried daughters, and saw nothing to impress him still. Since none had made overtures of friendship toward Daisy or her friends—or any women with far lower dowries—he kept his greetings on the cool side.

After half an hour of his indifference, the hostess was finally exasperated by his lack of interest in debutants and gave up. She excused herself and told him to enjoy the party.

He *would*, now that she had stopped trying to saddle him with unsuitable women while preventing him from even speaking with Daisy.

He made his way around the room again and, as hoped, came upon Daisy. She looked as frustrated as he felt. He bowed, and they made small talk for a moment.

"I was beginning to think we wouldn't have a chance to speak tonight," Daisy observed.

"Lady Sanderson is an old friend and means well." He regarded Daisy, including the low-cut gown she was wearing, and then tugged on his neckcloth.

"She wishes to see you matched quickly and claim the credit, I suppose. I'm surprised she let you escape her clutches so soon."

"Foolishness," he complained. The only woman who interested him was within arm's reach now. He inched closer to Daisy and lowered his voice. "I thought, perhaps, I shouldn't make it obvious I was eager to talk to you."

Daisy smiled and kept her eyes on the crowd. "I feel the same. Is it not strange."

"Yes," he agreed.

Max was more comfortable with his attraction to Daisy when they were alone. Here, he had to guard every word and gesture from others standing nearby. They were already drawing attention. "Perhaps we could take a turn about the room and talk some more?"

"I should like that," she said, and they turned away from the hostess. She did not reach for his arm, and he did not offer it, either. After a few steps, she glanced up at him. "My lord, I'm curious about something. Why do you *really* not wish to inherit the dukedom?"

Max nodded. "For so many reasons. The distance from London is one, the drafty halls and freezing winters there another. The bowing and simpering that started tonight, when I walked into the ballroom as a future duke. The worry and expense of maintaining so large an estate, and the debts I will likely inherit upon my uncle's demise. Also, my cousin spent money unwisely in expectation of his eventual elevation, leaving his widow poor, and it's likely the ducal estate will have to pay her bills, too, just to avoid the scandal of it all."

"Lord Throsby, you have always worried a great deal too much, but I'm sure you'll rise to the challenge and succeed beyond your wildest dreams," Daisy promised, and her smile suggested utter confidence in him.

He felt his cheeks heating from the unexpected praise and support that had been so rare in his adult life. "I'll do my best not to disappoint you."

"You didn't approve of him, did you? Your cousin, I mean."

Gerald had been lazy, using his position as heir presumptive to get his way and spending money in the same fashion. "I did not approve of many of his decisions, no."

Daisy shivered, then pulled her shawl tightly around her. "And yet he still made you guardian to his children."

"Someone had to be, and I suppose I was an easy choice, since I had experience with you. But it was most likely because he hated me and wished to burden me with a responsibility I couldn't escape."

Daisy sighed and then whispered, "Did you hate my father for making you my guardian?"

"Your father died before I even knew about the guardianship. Cursing him in his grave was the best I could manage," he said with a wry grin.

"I did that, too." Daisy winced before subtly turning him toward the supper room. There were already dishes set out in readiness for the break in the dancing, but the chamber was more or less empty save for servants setting out platters. "So, you will become a duke one day. You'll have to start preparing for it now, of course."

"I'd like to know how I'm to do that?"

Daisy approached a table and helped herself to two small sandwiches. Max followed and added four to his plate, plus a pastry. She headed for a table for two set against a far wall and sat without waiting for his assistance.

He joined her immediately.

As he studied Daisy, the simple act of eating together turned into a pleasurable pursuit. Her sigh of delight when the sandwich met her high expectations amused him, as it had so many times before.

"These are so good I could eat a dozen," she confessed. "How old are your new wards?"

"Quite young. Both under five." He gobbled up the first sandwich in two bites but took longer with the second and third. "Delicious, indeed."

Daisy beamed and picked up her second. "They will need a governess soon, and one who can provide them with an education that matches their future and the lesser position in society they will occupy. After all, they can no longer be groomed to be a future duke's offspring."

"That is true," Max added, eating in silence for a moment. "The pastries are good, too," he promised, and went to fetch another pair. He offered one to Daisy, but she declined. "What else do I need to think about?"

Daisy sat forward. "The widow."

Max tensed. "What about her?"

"If you don't marry her, or want her under your roof when you *do* marry, you must provide a home for her and the children elsewhere. Perhaps you should bring her to London."

"She did suggest coming to London in yesterdays letter."

Daisy's eyes widened. "She wrote to you again?"

He frowned sourly. "It seems to have become a daily event."

"She is panicking about her future, most likely. Afraid she'll be cast out, should you marry. When will that be?"

He gave her a sideways glance and then looked around the room to see who was near. The room had begun to fill while they sat together talking. There were far too many ears around now to discuss his exact plans with her. He'd already said too much in public as it was. "We should discuss that later and somewhere with fewer ears."

Daisy finally glanced around and, seeing people watching them too, nodded. Even more people were drifting into the room now in groups, regarding them with great interest.

She stood abruptly. "I'd best go before the gossips get wind of our affair," she said quietly. Then louder, "And I really must offer my compliments to Lady Sanderson on the pleasure of her supper tonight. It was a pleasure to speak with you again, Lord Throsby, and thank you for answering my questions. I do hope you enjoy what remains of the ball."

He inclined his head but was stunned by her abrupt decision to end their talk. He'd been enjoying listening to her voice again. He lowered his own voice to a whisper. "I doubt it could be as enjoyable as being alone with you."

A soft smile appeared upon her lips, but she went on her

way quickly, back to the ballroom and any other suitors she might not have told him about. Max watched her go, but then noticed *he* was being watched by other women, too.

A few smiled as if encouraged by his solitude. He finished his food and stood, making his way out of the supper room, heading back to the ballroom, though he kept a distance from Daisy now. He did not want to presume upon her time. He also did not want anyone to notice his interest.

But he couldn't tear his eyes away from her for long. The way she laughed, spoke with others, and danced fascinated him. He'd not planned for it, certainly not expected to crave being in her company so much. The woman had done all she could to pick fights with him over the years.

That was probably why he admired her so much now. She'd not backed down just because he'd had total control of her life. She'd not cowered, or simpered, or tried to weasel her way into his good graces. She'd wanted, *demanded* to be seen as his equal.

Until now, he'd felt he needed to stand apart from her. Set a good example. But now he was *not* her guardian, and that need to behave appropriately at all times had diminished. He knew what he wanted and needed. But he could not simply take it or assume. He had to earn her favor, and by degrees.

He turned his back on Daisy, watching the other guests come and go from the ballroom, but soon became aware of a figure standing close by. When he turned to acknowledge the person, he discovered Miss Justine Dawes had snuck up beside him.

And the girl was unmarried.

Daisy and Justine were not on speaking terms still, but

he was certain Daisy would not want her former friend to be snubbed, even when all he wanted to do was run back to the safety of Daisy's company. "Miss Dawes. A pleasure to see you again."

"Lord Throsby," she murmured. "It's been too long."

"Yes. All of a day," he murmured, growing alarmed with the way she toyed with her dance card. "You should know that the item you dropped was retrieved. Once cleaned, it will be returned to your possession."

Miss Dawes gulped, and her dance card dropped from her fingers. "You should not have troubled yourself on my behalf."

"I did what Miss Ellis would have wanted me to do. You are her friend."

"Those days are over," she whispered sadly.

Max did not want to encourage a girl who might consider him husband material, because surely she must know how Daisy had thought of him as a guardian. "Perhaps they are not, after all. Miss Ellis is here tonight. Perhaps you could speak to her about the book and arrange to receive it from her hand instead of mine."

Justine turned to look at him in alarm. "Has she read it?"

"The book has not been read by her and will not be read by anyone," he promised.

"Thank you," she whispered, and then exhaled sharply.

He glanced across the gathering and spotted Daisy watching him and Justine together, her expression arrested. He inclined his head but turned to Miss Dawes. "Have you been well?"

"Yes, my lord."

"Happy?"

Justine swallowed but did not answer, not that he blamed her. He had never been a lady's first choice for confidant.

Daisy could get anyone to talk about their feelings. Even him. Miss Dawes had once confided in her, too. But the young woman had been skirting the edges of dance floors since her sister's abrupt marriage to Lord Brookes, barely speaking to anyone, and not enjoying herself as she once appeared to do in Daisy's company.

He glanced across at Daisy and raised a brow. Daisy answered with a tiny nod, and he turned to Miss Dawes. "I've always found it easier to get a difficult task done quickly. Saves endless worry about the result."

"I don't understand."

He pursed his lips a moment, debating the wisdom of getting involved. "You'd like to talk to her, and she'd like to talk to you. I suggest you take the direct approach. Daisy doesn't hold grudges, and I believe she has missed you very much."

Justine made an odd noise, glanced around, and then excused herself in a hurry. He watched her go, frowning, and realized his suggestion had upset her.

Justine's sister strolled past him, giving him a deathly stare as she followed after her sister.

Daisy walked toward him next, shaking her head when she stopped. "I see your tact remains unchanged, Lord Throsby."

"That is probably true," he agreed after a moment. But all he'd done was suggest Miss Dawes gather her courage and talk to her old friend. He hadn't expected his words to inspire such distress.

"Well?"

"Well." He glanced at the dance card dangling from her wrist. "Who are you to dance with next?"

"No one. I am leaving."

"It's a little early."

She smiled. "The night is still young, and I'm expecting a friend to visit me at my home tonight."

Max was shocked—until he noticed the wicked sparkle in her eye. *He* was the friend Daisy was expecting to meet with tonight. To say he was aroused by her bold invitation was an understatement, but reacting to that here was dangerous for her reputation.

He glanced around the room as if he was bored, greatly relieved no one paid them the slightest bit of attention now.

When he glanced down at Daisy again, and his heart swelled with anticipation. "Yes, well, you should go home so your friend can visit you as soon as possible. He is rather impatient to have you all to himself again."

"Until later, then," she whispered, inclining her head regally, but her excitement was palpable and infectious.

Daisy swept out of the ballroom, an obvious spring in her steps, at least to him. He groaned under his breath as she glanced over her shoulder before finally disappearing. He wanted to follow her immediately and travel in the same carriage. He would pull her into his arms in the dark confines and kiss her witless if given the chance. This slow courtship he'd planned might kill him, the way she flirted with him so effortlessly.

Max counted to ten, and then twenty, before he strolled for the front door to have his carriage called. Although eager to catch up with Daisy and sweep her off her feet, he would do nothing to damage the reputation of a future duchess.

He had his carriage drop him some distance from her home, and only when it was gone did he turn for the welcoming light of her small town house windows and run up her front steps to knock.

Chapter Eleven

Daisy wrenched open the front door of her town house as soon as she heard the first tap upon the old wooden surface. Throsby stood on her doorstep, looking flustered, impatient, and so proper in his familiar evening clothes. Daisy ushered him inside and closed the door to keep the world at bay for the night.

"Where is Gibbs?" Throsby asked immediately, looking around anxiously.

Daisy turned and leaned against the heavy locked door, her breath coming fast. "Sent to bed."

Throsby took a step in her direction. "Was he suspicious?"

"If he was, I never noticed." Daisy had been too excited about her midnight caller, and delighted that Throsby had readily agreed to come, to worry about what her devoted and well-paid butler might think. She wet her lips. "Shall we adjourn to the sitting room?"

"I'll go anywhere you want," he promised, and held out his hand to her.

Daisy took it and tugged him into the adjoining room.

Throsby shut the door behind them and turned to her, one brow raised. But instead of a frown, there was a smile on his lips. Gods, he was a handsome devil when he smiled.

She couldn't wait to feel his hands on her body again and his lips pressed against hers, but he was too far away still.

She moved toward him, swaying her hips a little, and the smile slipped from his face.

"Miss Ellis."

"Call me Daisy again," she said softly, giving him the permission she could have given him years ago.

"This is not a good idea," he warned, digging a finger under his collar and pulling at it hard.

She loved his reaction to her little teasing strut and caught up his hand to squeeze his fingers. "I think it's the best I've ever had."

Daisy drew him close, caught him by the cravat, and looked him in the eye. Their bodies were barely touching, but the tension between them increased, now they were alone.

She had never felt this way with any of the gentlemen who'd called on her or even stolen a brief kiss. Certainly, none of the ones she'd hidden under tables had caused her heart to race so fast.

She stretched up, pursing her lips in anticipation of a kiss.

Throsby slowly lowered his head but only pressed his forehead against hers. He let his breath out slowly. "There are a thousand reasons why I shouldn't have come."

"I can think of only why you should have," she whispered and brought his hand to her waist, loving the sound of his immediate groan.

She released his fingers and watched as he caressed her body through the gown. The material made a delicious wispy sound as his rough fingers moved higher. His hand finally settled on the top of her shoulder.

"What have I warned you about wearing gowns like this?"

"You claimed they inspired lust in gentlemen," she whispered and puffed out her chest a little more. "Is that true for you, too?"

He didn't answer, but eased the gown off her shoulder and dragged his finger along her skin until he reached the top of one breast…and then slipped it under the top of her low-cut bodice. "Yes."

Daisy's let out a shuddering breath.

He turned his attention to her other shoulder and the bit of fabric there. He also eased it aside and then downward. The only thing holding her gown up was her bosom now.

Throsby had to know that.

His breath churned.

Daisy almost couldn't breathe as he set his hands on her waist and applied a gentle downward pressure against the gown, making the garment fall to her hips.

Max kissed her hard, and Daisy kissed him back with equal fervor, delighting in the sensation of her bare breasts pressed against his properly clothed body.

He got a hand between them and cupped her breast. Squeezing and thumbing her nipple languidly. Throsby swallowed her cries of astonishment at how good it felt when he pinched hard.

"Throsby…"

"Yes, Minx?" he murmured.

She gaped, affronted by the term. "Minx?"

He laughed softly and removed his hands from her. "I

have called you that in my mind since the day you threw a vase at my head and stormed out of the room in a right royal huff over the guardianship. You hated me that day, and I could not blame you. I was angry with *you*, too."

"I did not believe I needed you," she answered, hands on her hips, irritated that he was speaking of the past again.

He cocked his head to one side and held her gaze a long moment before he spoke. "Do you *need* me now?"

She felt the question like a stroke across her skin. Did she need Throsby? She certainly wanted him to keep kissing her and touching her breasts. He'd started something with their first kiss, and she wanted more and more of him each time they were alone. She wanted him in a way she hardly understood.

But he was not someone she had to obey without question now. The choices were still hers to make, including whether to see this through to the inevitable conclusion. He was giving her time to change her mind about their affair.

They were becoming intimate with each other by the day. They had started making love tonight. She wanted more of that. More of the thrill, and to learn the inevitable finish with him. She had educated herself as far as she could on how ladies and men found pleasure with each other, but she was out of her depth now.

Throsby waited, a look of pure patience on his face. He would let her stop without question, she was sure of that.

Daisy took him by the hand and led him to the settee. She pushed him down and placed herself primly on his knee.

"Should I take that as a yes?" he asked, the corners of his mouth turning up again into a knowing smile.

"Yes, you should."

Throsby drew her closer, buried his face against her throat, and kissed her there. A shiver raced through her whole body as he adjusted her into a comfortable position in his arms and resumed kissing her again with a gentle passion that kept her coming back for more.

While they kissed, Daisy toyed with his neckcloth, discovering how it came undone, and slowly dragged it from his neck before undoing the top button on his fine linen shirt.

Throsby groaned as she slid her hand under the linen, touching his body for the first time, and then he lifted her up to bury his face between her breasts and kiss them.

Daisy squirmed on his lap, and he set her back down, but she'd only been seeking greater contact. He did not need to overpower her with his strength to prove himself desirable.

She ran her hands over any part of his body she could reach, loving the frantic quality of his indrawn breaths.

Suddenly, she was on her back with Throsby hovering above her, her hands pinned beneath his. He had his weight supported by his arms, but his lower half pressed hard against her sex.

It felt good, and clearly, Throsby was aroused by what they had done together so far. She looked up into his eyes and smiled, relieved he felt the same thrill. She anticipated that her satisfaction would be better than any of her wicked imaginings had ever conjured up.

He brushed his hips against hers, then pressed a little harder. Daisy's breath shuddered in response to the feel of his cock straining toward her. He rocked against her a few times, watching her face closely.

Daisy couldn't look away and widened her legs without prompting, seeking more of the thrilling sensation. Throsby paused, though, and reached for her leg. She expected him to raise her skirts immediately, but all he did was grasp her ankle and stroke his thumb across her ankle bone.

He chuckled, and she realized why he found her leg so amusing.

"Silk stockings," she whispered.

"Only the best for a minx."

"I did not buy them for you," she explained.

"Perhaps not, but you have enjoyed torturing me with those brief glimpses of you wearing them, haven't you?"

"I flashed my ankles because I expected it would drive you out of the house," she admitted with a wince of discomfort.

"I know." He leaned down to whisper in her ear. "Now, when you flash your stockings at me, all I will want to do is fall to my knees at your feet. Hardly dignified behavior, but it's the risk you'll take in the future, Minx, when you tease an ardent admirer."

It was quite odd to hear Throsby speak of desire so casually. It was also vastly flattering that she might provoke such a response from him. "In a lover, I would encourage such worship," she teased.

Throsby nodded. "As you wish."

He drew back immediately, moving off the settee until he was kneeling at her side. She leaned up to protest the loss of his body against hers, but then Throsby kissed the top of her foot and she laughed softly.

He gently removed her slipper and held her foot aloft in his hand, looking at it. And then he resumed kissing her, from the tip of her toes to the hem of her gown. Daisy's breath caught each time he raised her skirt one inch after another, dropping unhurried kisses until he reached the ribbon she used as a garter at her knee.

He untied the bow with his teeth and set the ribbon aside.

And then he rolled down her stocking and stripped it away from her leg.

"I take it you don't like silk stockings, after all?"

"It was in my way," he promised before kissing her bare toes and then back up to her knee again. Daisy shivered with every kiss, every brush of lips, every breath against her skin. She thought she might combust should he kiss higher.

He did.

Her legs were already parted, and there was nothing but her flimsy gown and petticoat to impede his progress higher and higher. His lips were nearing the top of her thighs when he paused, panting hot against her thigh. "I want to keep kissing you until the end, Daisy. Do you understand? May I continue?"

She knew what his request would entail. He wanted to know her intimately. She'd overheard a widow whisper of wicked things done to her by a lover, and she'd thought of that as she'd achieved a release in her own bed many times. Throsby could use his mouth on her body to bring her undone. It was an intimacy she'd not expected, yet wanted to experience now with him.

She nodded. "You can do anything you want with me."

He clucked his tongue. "That is not something you should offer a scoundrel so freely. I want quite a lot."

She laughed and threaded her fingers through his hair. "I trust you not to get carried away."

"I will do my best for you."

"You always have," she admitted, realizing that she deeply admired Throsby's dependability. He had never truly let her down. He would not tonight, either.

She closed her eyes as his kisses resumed, and he held her legs apart. But her eyes flashed open again as he dropped a kiss directly onto her curls.

Then her mouth opened in a soundless wail as he parted her lower lips with his thumbs and kissed her hard down there.

It was torture!

It was bliss!

She squirmed and wriggled and thrust her hips up into his face at the pleasurable torment he provided her. And yet that still wasn't close enough to bring her to release.

She gripped his hair, and when he kissed a spot so incredibly sensitive, she held his head firmly to that place. She felt the flick of his tongue and the suction of his mouth, and her back arched, pushing her sex hard against him in search of her climax.

She came suddenly, silently, and crashed down afterward, spent and blissfully stunned.

Throsby's mouth softened against her before he turned his face slightly to rest his cheek upon her bare inner thigh, gasping for breath himself. She toyed with his hair, enjoying the sensation of it slipping through her fingers. But her heart fluttered as she looked down upon his head. He was the last man she'd ever imagined making love to her or developing deeper feelings for.

Somehow, Throsby had carved out a place in her affections and her future. She could not believe he would toy with her feelings with no thought for the consequences.

What astonished Daisy, though, is that any future with him near did not trouble her at all now. She knew what challenges his future held in store. He would do well as a duke, as the head of his family, and as her lover. He did everything to the best of his ability.

She tousled his hair, smiling. "Are you comfortable?"

"Are you?"

"Yes," she promised. "But perhaps you could come up here and lie upon me. I'm ready."

"Not tonight," Throsby said, as he moved to lie beside her, and then he pulled her close against his side. He kissed her brow, and then settled with a deep sigh and his hand covering her breast. "I've already been here too long."

"I wish you could stay," she whispered.

"I will one day soon," he promised.

Although disappointed that he had to go, she accepted his decision. But Daisy didn't want to move out of his arms yet and cuddled closer to him.

Throsby was solid and warm and familiar. He had hidden his passionate nature so very well. His tenderness and consideration had been everything she ever dreamed of from a man she might love.

Although her breath caught at that thought, she let it out slowly because the idea of someone loving Throsby wasn't as preposterous as she'd always imagined.

She likely *did* love him already.

Why else would she be so easily swept off her feet? Why else let him back into her life so eagerly? She'd well and truly ruined herself with the man. Everyone in society would say so, and yet he was letting her take her time getting used to him and the increasing intimacy between them.

He was a good man, the kind she'd always dreamed of marrying one day. Someone dependable, someone kind, someone who liked her just as she was—well, almost. Someone who would put her needs first, the way he already had.

Someone who desired her like no other.

There was only one thing wrong with Throsby. He still did not smile often enough. Something had to be done about that before they eventually wed.

Chapter Twelve

There was nothing worse than being a man with a grand future ahead of him when he had never wanted or expected it. It made him a target for false flattery, winsome looks, and bold invitations to share a lady's bed in exchange for the expectation of gaining a title for themselves. However, the minx Max wanted to flirt with him wasn't currently around.

Daisy appeared not to have been invited to tonight's ball after all, and he was growing cross about that because the hostess had mentioned Daisy by name when he had first arrived.

He was torn about what to do. Leave early and visit her at home, remain in case Daisy was delayed, or wait until tomorrow to make a call as a proper suitor ought to do.

While together, he understood Daisy and his feelings. When apart, his doubts returned. It was still hard to forget how difficult their time together as guardian and ward had been. He wasn't sure enough time had passed to erase the memory of him behaving like a pompous, cold prig toward her.

But distance had been necessary then. If he'd let down his guard he might have liked her too much, and come to care about her too soon, and those were not feelings a guardian should ever have developed for a ward they had to give away to another man.

He had those feelings now. He had slowly, grudgingly, admitted to himself that he'd fallen for the most exasperating woman he'd ever met. He wanted to see her smile at him the way she had been doing lately. He wanted to see her face as she climaxed again and again.

He turned away from the dance floor, kept his gaze down so he did not see the inviting glances, and headed for the refreshment table. From there, he might catch a glimpse of Daisy arriving in the entrance hall more clearly.

"Throsby!"

Max turned his head and spied the recently married Duke of Mamble bearing down on him. "Your grace. I hadn't heard you had returned to Town."

Mamble stretched out his hand to shake. "Just today. My wife insisted on attending tonight's ball and is somewhere about, no doubt already whispering in her dear friend Miss Ellis' ear. We brought her with us tonight. I hope you don't object."

"I've no objections, of course," he promised, as his heart began to race. Daisy was here somewhere. He looked around for her or the Duchess of Mamble, but he didn't see either one nearby, unfortunately.

He turned his attention back to the duke when the man cleared his throat.

"It's good of you, given the circumstances," the duke murmured.

"Circumstances?"

"I did not agree with the way Miss Ellis evicted you. Damn shoddy of her, but I only learned of what she'd intended after it was too late."

Max nodded. "To be honest, it's no longer a source of

strife between us. We both spoke our minds that night. Cleared the air, as it were. She is no longer my responsibility, and I am no longer considered her enemy."

Mamble's breath rushed out. "I am particularly relieved to hear that."

"Oh? Why?"

"Well, you must know there are few in London I can tolerate for long. You have become a good friend, and I can always count on you to talk sense."

Max was surprised to hear he'd made that much of an impression. He'd hardly spent that much time with the duke…but should he and Daisy marry, a friendship with the duke would certainly make nights like this more pleasant. "I trust your travels were uneventful."

"Yes, the roads were as expected, accommodations acceptable, and I enjoyed several nights of uninterrupted pleasure—"

"Please don't finish that sentence," Max begged, afraid the duke would launch into a description of their intimate marital adventures.

Mamble laughed. "I was going to say of *stargazing* with my wife. Her grace enjoyed the outdoors and the change of scenery from London very much, but she missed her dear friend too much to stay away for long."

"I am sure she was also much missed," Max promised.

Mamble glanced around and leaned closer to whisper, "Miss Ellis actually squealed when we arrived unannounced at her door today. I've never heard such a sound before."

Max chuckled softly. "I am well acquainted with that habit and sound. They were close from the day they met."

"My wife wants to take Miss Ellis home with us, and

keep her there for Christmas, too." Mamble drew closer still. "I gather the girl's not made a match while we've been gone from Town?"

"Not that I've heard of, but I have not spent much time in society these past weeks." Max wet his lips nervously. If invited, Daisy was sure to want to go away with her friend to the countryside to see where the duchess would live, which would interfere with his slow courtship of the minx. "When were you thinking of leaving?"

"A date has not been set, but soon, I should think," Mamble said, as he looked around. "Gods, I hate the way people stare and whisper."

"Every gentleman does. Ignore them," he said, as he spied Lord and Lady Brookes sweeping into the room. The lady smiled while the man, Brookes, seemed to be perspiring heavily. He watched the man mop his face and hastily accept a glass of champagne.

Tonight, Max did not see Miss Dawes trailing immediately behind them, which was unusual. He ought to somehow report to her that he had her book recovered to pristine condition. Daisy was to deliver it though, but she could not if she was taken from Town.

He had to ensure Daisy might stay in Town for a little longer.

Max turned back to whisper to the duke, "She might have one suitor."

"Oh, who?"

"I'd rather not say," he hedged, knowing the danger of going too far with his tale. But he could not have Daisy spirited away from London before he had a chance and time to make a proper offer. "I'd keep it to yourself for now."

"Of course." Mamble frowned. "I'm sure my wife will discover who he might be, and perhaps we can help speed things in the right direction."

Max shuffled his feet. He didn't need help, he needed time. Marriage would last a lifetime. He wanted Daisy to consider him properly, in her own time, and not to have any regrets later. He didn't want to rush her to the altar just to fit with anyone's schedule but her own.

"Lord Throsby! What a surprise to see you here tonight," the Duchess of Mamble said, pulling him from his thoughts as she appeared beside her husband. A tense smile was fixed in place as she extended her hand toward him.

He bowed over it. "Your grace. A pleasure to have you back in London. We missed you."

She looked at him in confusion, tilting her head—and that movement revealed Daisy, who had been standing slightly behind her friend and out of immediate sight.

She stepped out of the duchess's shadow, revealing a daring gown he'd refused to let her wear in public during the guardianship. The fabric was too sheer, and the bodice was cut too low not to have scoundrels flocking to feast on the view.

As a guardian, he would have dragged Daisy from the ball immediately for daring to defy his instructions. However, as her smitten lover, his first thought was to find a secluded alcove where he could kiss her witless and peel her out of it.

He dragged his eyes up from her body with difficulty. Daisy extended her hand, looking at him in a way that suggested she'd worn the dress just to irk him and was trying not to laugh at his reaction. The minx was aware that he struggled to ignore her appeal now, and she was secretly delighted by his reaction to the forbidden gown.

"Miss Ellis," he ground out.

"Lord Throsby," she crooned. "It's been too long."

Thirteen hours or so. He had slipped from her home just as the sun was rising, while she slept. He took up her hand and squeezed it a little harder than he would with other women, to let her know he knew her game. "It has."

"Daisy was just telling me the sad news about your cousin. I am so sorry for your loss," the duchess interjected in a lowered voice, edging between them. She glanced down.

Max dropped Daisy's hand when he realized he'd kept hold of it. "Thank you, your grace."

"What's all this?" Mamble asked, and his wife whispered the news of his future elevation.

Mamble caught his eye. "Now we will have even more to talk about."

"I suppose we will," Max agreed.

"I'm surprised to see you here tonight, though," the duchess cut in, keeping her voice low. "I thought you would be with your family in the country."

Daisy whispered in the duchess's ear, and after a moment, she nodded and backed away. "I understand." Then Mamble wrapped the duchess' arm through his, and she nodded. "Well, I'm afraid we must leave you, my lord. I hope you enjoy your evening. Come along, Daisy."

"In a moment," Daisy said quickly. "I need to ask Lord Throsby a question."

"Find us when you're done with him," the duchess requested.

Daisy nodded, but when the duchess turned away, she laughed softly and whispered, "That might be never."

Max felt something shift in his chest, and then swell. Hope. She wanted more of him. He checked who was standing nearby before he spoke. "How did you feel this morning?"

"It's hard to put into words," she murmured, nodding to a passerby.

"Horrified?"

"Hardly." She wet her lips and then turned to face the room. "Though I was surprised to wake up alone on the settee and properly dressed again."

"Discretion seemed appropriate, and I told you I would have to leave. You were impossible to wake, by the way."

"It was improper, wasn't it, inviting you home like that and trying to keep you there?"

He scowled rather than grin. "That wasn't the truly improper part."

"No." She fanned herself. "That part was fun."

"Fun?"

"Seeing you like that, after all these years of scowling at me, was a delightful change." She leaned a little closer, her breath coming fast. "You are just full of surprises lately, my lord."

Max wanted to smirk. He scowled again instead. "Would you care for further surprises from me?"

"I could bear it very easily," she whispered, and then her eyes fixed on a distant point in the room. She nodded and then looked up at him. "You still have your key, don't you?"

It was in his pocket now. He'd never gone anywhere

without it in years, but probably should have returned it long ago. "I do."

"Use it tonight when you follow me home. Do excuse me. The duchess calls."

She hurried across the room, away from him, to join the duchess and her circle. The pair immediately began to whisper again, and the duchess cast a worried glance in his direction. He'd seen them like that quite often, and although he was sure their conversation could be about him or some other scandalous thing, he wasn't as worried anymore about where such scheming might lead Daisy.

She'd begun whispering to *him* now, and he'd already been invited to visit Daisy tonight. Perhaps they would discuss the future, one where her friendship with the Duchess of Mamble couldn't come between them.

But that would be after he kissed her soundly. After he'd pinned her against the wall again and berated her for flaunting her breasts at him. He would only be satisfied again after he'd felt her small, delicate hands touch his skin. He could hardly wait for another chance to have her unbound from her gown and undone with pleasure. To excite her. Touch her body until she was panting his name again.

Throsby watched Daisy for as long as he dared and then realized he'd better mingle with the other guests before someone noticed his interest in her. He circulated, but he was counting the minutes until she left so he could leave, too. But it was far too early to go without offending the hostess.

Across the room, he caught Daisy watching him. The fingers of her right hand wriggled in an almost wave and a blush colored her cheeks. After a moment, she whispered to her friend and headed for the front hall. She glanced his way once, though, before exiting the ballroom.

Max followed discreetly, as he usually would have as her guardian, attempting to cut her off from meeting some swain under the stairs.

Daisy was waiting for him there, but then giggled and disappeared into a nearby room. Max checked for other guests lurking about before he followed her inside.

It was too dark to see anything but a pair of small hands reaching to capture his face before the door closed, and then his head was pulled downward. "I couldn't wait until later to kiss you. Don't muss my gown too badly," Daisy warned.

He smoothed his fingers over her cheeks, breathing hard. "I can make no promises about that, since you're wearing a gown I expressly forbid you to wear in public."

"I wore it just for you," she promised. "Knowing you would scowl so fiercely, driven mad by wanting me."

"I suspected that motive already," he whispered back, rather flattered though. "And yes, all I want to do is tear it from your body with my teeth."

"Later," Daisy said, and then kissed him hard on the lips.

Max lifted her from her feet, pressed her against the nearest wall, and made love to her mouth with unhurried delight.

But after a moment or two, he heard the distinct sound of floorboards creaking behind his back.

Max froze and shielded Daisy from being seen. "Get out," he ordered.

"I always said he liked you," a woman said.

Throsby struggled to place the voice. Female. Young. Acquainted with them both and oddly familiar.

Daisy shifted out from behind him and faced the speaker. "So you did, Miss Dawes. I was still surprised, though."

Max cursed softly but Daisy's fingers settled over his lips, silencing him.

"And it's clear to see you like him, too, now," Miss Dawes accused.

"Yes, it seems I do. Very much so," Daisy promised. Her hand moved to cup his jaw, and Max couldn't help but kiss her palm.

"I will leave you to it," Miss Dawes said.

"I appreciate that."

The door opened and closed, exposing them in a flash of light, and the young woman was gone.

Daisy leaned against him. "I wonder what Justine was doing hiding in a dark room?"

"Dear God, that's the least of our problems," he whispered in horror, drawing back from Daisy. Miss Dawes had been in the room when they'd come in and started making love, and she had not yet made up with Daisy. "Will she talk about us? Tell her sister. You never know what Lady Brookes will do and say about us."

"I don't know what *Justine* will do or say. She might wish to see my reputation in tatters over this." Daisy's hand settled on his cheek again. "Not to worry, darling. We can deal with that later."

"Daisy, you cannot ignore—"

She shut him up with a long, heated kiss. Just when he thought they'd make love here, Daisy let him up for air and hugged him. "Stop worrying and rejoin me in the ballroom soon," she whispered.

Then she disappeared from the room, leaving him with a thousand questions and even more worries. The last thing he wanted was trouble right now for either of them. Not when her reputation and good standing in society were at stake.

Max stood about, uncertain of what to do or how long to wait to return to the ballroom. He never imagined he might be the one who ruined Daisy.

And then he recalled something odd. Daisy had called him *darling*.

It took him ten minutes to wipe the smile off his face, but by then, Daisy was dancing with an unworthy swain.

Justine Dawes was nowhere to be seen.

He breathed easy only after he'd done a full circuit of the ballroom and halls and hadn't found her sister or Lord Brookes there, either.

No one looked at him strangely or whispered about him or Daisy as he passed by. He spoke to Daisy after she left the dance floor a second time but made certain not to linger too long in her vicinity, even though he wanted to enjoy her flirting with him. However, there was only so much of that he could bear before he reacted to it, and that might be disastrous.

He only took his leave when Daisy was headed for home in the duke's large carriage with the duke and duchess, very late in the morning.

Chapter Thirteen

Daisy was sitting up in bed under the sheets by the time Throsby finally let himself into her home. She listened to him move about, almost breathless as he finally made his way up the stairs to her door. When he stepped into her bedchamber, she was almost overcome with impatience to kiss him again.

He stopped dead still when he saw her waiting in bed, and then approached slowly, stopping at the foot. His gaze swept over her bare shoulders and then flickered to the floor, where her chemise lay discarded, then seemed to look about again, clearly for the gown she'd worn earlier that evening.

His expression was one of disappointment. "Sorry to have kept you waiting so long."

She shrugged, letting her sheet slip a little lower. "You are much later than I expected."

"Discretion," he replied. "I feared it would seem odd if I left soon after you did."

Now that Throsby was here, discretion was the furthest thing from Daisy's mind. She wanted to continue where they had left off the night before. She'd thought about Throsby all day, and it made perfect sense now why she had disliked having a guardian.

All her agitation over him and the guardianship had a reason. She might have liked him, but she hadn't been *allowed* to. But that didn't matter anymore. The rules, her reputation. She was going to give up her life as she knew it for something much better.

Women always did when they found the men they'd lost their hearts to.

She would marry Throsby as soon as it was convenient and live together again. He could stomp through the halls as much as he liked, and she'd just flash her stockings at him and wear scandalous dresses to drive him wild.

Everything would work out in the end.

Tonight, her servants had been warned to ignore any odd noises they might hear, and besides, they were fond of Throsby anyway. They might not even be shocked if they found him naked in her bed when morning came. They had always wanted to keep him under this roof. Daisy did, too, now.

"You were unusually light-footed when you came in tonight. You always charged through the house like a bull at a gate before."

He shrugged. "Only so you heard me and had time to hide your beaus or pretend to read the paper I would ask for."

She smiled brightly, glad her efforts to irritate him had been noticed. "I'm not pretending with you or hiding anything anymore." She let the sheet fall to expose her breasts and glanced at the bulge in his trousers. "What's hidden under there fills me with great curiosity, by the way."

He grinned but leaned against the bedpost rather than come closer. "We should talk first."

She pouted, and wrapping her arms about her bent

knees. "Why? Are you going to lecture me about my gowns or propriety again?"

"Not exactly."

"I know things. There's no need to worry. I'll not be shocked when we make love," she promised.

"That wasn't ever my concern, but it does confirm my suspicions about you. Now, about Justine."

She sighed. He wanted to discuss their indiscretion and Justine spotting them. Things might have changed between them, but he was still very much the same man who'd worried about her reputation all season. "Justine will talk or not talk about us. There are no guarantees she'd keep a secret now, if she ever would have before."

"Do you realize the way you talked tonight suggested there was an understanding between us?" he said.

"I guess I did."

"You said you liked me."

"I *do* like you. Come here, darling, and kiss me again," she said, stretching out her arms to him and wiggling her fingers in her impatience for a kiss that could not be interrupted.

Throsby wagged a finger at her. "There's that strange word again. Darling?"

"Do you dislike hearing it?"

"It is unexpected."

"I don't see why it should be. I've heard women call their lovers such all the time."

He glanced around her room. "So, where's the gown?"

"Hidden away somewhere safe."

"Safe?"

"I won't let you tear it up or give it away because you think it too scandalous for me to wear."

He straightened and came around to the side of the bed, looking serious. "I wouldn't do that now. I was hoping to help you slip out of it. I'd wanted to do that since I saw you wearing it tonight."

Daisy grinned, delighted by his reaction to the forbidden gown. Since she was bare under the sheets, bare from head to knee, he'd already seen quite a lot of her. But she'd left her stockings on just for him, though he couldn't know that yet. "I wanted to be sure you could not mistake my intentions with you."

"I've never misunderstood you."

"But you get very cross, very often."

"Frustrated," he corrected. "You enjoyed making my life difficult."

"I'm sorry," she whispered.

"Don't be. It's in the past." Her breath caught as Throsby slipped off his coat and undid one button on his waistcoat, and then another. "Tell me, is there an understanding between us now, *Daisy*?"

"I think there must be, *Max*. Or I could stick with darling," she suggested with a bright smile.

"Only as long as you promise to marry me one day, Minx," he murmured.

"One day?"

"I do not want you to rush your decision about us. That is why I have not taken anything for granted about you."

Daisy cocked her head to the side and realized Max was quite nervous about them, when there was no need. She had chosen well for her husband. Max was exciting and surprising—now the tedious guardianship business was out of the way. He would not lead her on and break her heart.

He'd claimed it.

She rose up onto her knees, exposing her nakedness. "I would prefer some rush tonight, if you don't mind. Any moment I could be an old maid."

"You're just the right age for me," he promised, as he took a step closer, his gaze sweeping her from head to knee, then he glanced around her to her feet. "Just how many pairs of those do you own by now?"

"Oh, dozens and dozens. The purchases seemed to irritate you when the bills came, so I kept buying more, even after you were gone, though I suppose they won't irritate you anymore."

"Well, no." He drew closer, and his fingers brushed her hips lightly, and her breath caught. "Thinking of you wearing them, and like this, will only ever arouse me."

Daisy looped her arms about his neck and pressed her naked body against his. "My lord, we are done with irritation and have moved on to the more exciting part of our relationship. Please try to keep up."

He cupped her face, staring at her with such an odd look that she blushed. "Would you care to take off my clothes, Daisy?"

"I thought you'd never ask, Max."

"Will you also marry me once I've procured a special license?"

"Yes, Max, I will marry you, but before we head off to visit your family to break the news, there is something I need to do. I need to speak with Justine. Alone. Talk to her and ask what is going on. Hiding in dark rooms isn't like her."

"All right, our journey can wait for that conversation. But our marriage cannot be put off forever if I share your bed tonight. I'll want to return too often." He frowned. "I also heard the Duchess of Mamble plans to take you away with them soon."

"I'm not going anywhere you're not invited." She pushed his waistcoat away and then glanced down at the bulge in his trousers. "Not when you need me to take care of *that*. And, yes, we have an understanding. We're going to marry and be very happy together."

"We will."

He bent her backward and sealed their lips together in a kiss that took her breath away. She tugged his shirt out of his trousers in her impatience to feel his naked body close. Max pulled it over his head and tossed it aside carelessly. She had a brief chance to admire his muscled chest before he kissed her again, and she became lost in the wonder of making love.

Tonight, she was done with half measures and waiting though. She turned him under her the first chance she got.

From the dominant position over him, she surveyed her prize. Max was a well-built man, hairy-chested and oh so warm. She let her fingers dance over his skin, making sure no part of his torso was neglected.

"You really are all mine now," she told him.

"And you are mine," he warned, before flipping her over and pinning her down.

He raised her hands above her head and held them there. She squirmed, putting up a faint resistance, but she was exactly where she wanted to be.

Max nibbled her neck, and she squirmed in earnest then and he released her hands. "Do you never stay still?"

She fumbled with the buttons of his breeches. "Well, perhaps you're not holding the right part of me down yet," she taunted.

He adjusted, pinning down her hips with his own. Now, he was almost where she wanted him. She pushed at his breeches and then parted her legs and wrapped them around his hips.

"I always thought..."

"What?"

"I always feared my wife would end up being a model of decorum. Dull." He shoved his clothing lower and then thrust against her, once, twice, until the tip of his cock became wedged in a place that felt so good. So right. "Happy to be so wrong about that, too."

He pressed into her, holding her down as they became one. Daisy squirmed, seeking more of him inside her.

His hands cradled her face suddenly. "Don't be so impatient, love, or I'll hurt you."

He withdrew and pressed forward again. Daisy hadn't the heart to tell him she'd toyed with her own body so often, she was not feeling any pain at all.

Max held himself above her, not even thrusting, and grinned again. "There now. Well and truly ruined and all mine."

She narrowed her eyes at him. "I know that's not all there is to it."

Max rolled them with a husky laugh. "If you must have all me immediately, who am I to stand in your way? Ride me."

Daisy understood the request, and thought she knew the mechanics of making love. She was not about to let her lack of experience make her shy now. She positioned herself, knees bent, keeping him inside her, and attempted to move awkwardly up and down on his length.

Max grasped her hips and guided her movements, until she discovered a smooth, comfortable rhythm.

It was intoxicating, having Max heighten her pleasure in a way her own fingers and imagination could never achieve. She watched him. Noticed the sweat on his face and the flex of his body under hers as he enjoyed her efforts. She could feel her climax closing in, and twisted her hips, searching for the perfect pressure spot to send her over the edge.

Max finally touched her breasts, pinched her nipples between his fingers, and her back arched at the pleasure of that unexpected pain. She climaxed, crying out wordlessly, coming to a shuddering halt with Max still buried deep inside her.

When she met his gaze, she saw his jaw was locked tight. Every muscle of his body stiff.

"Max?"

"Wait."

"Max..."

He flipped her over, pinned her hands above her head again, and thrust. *Hard.* "Forgive me, I can't stop."

Daisy wrenched her hands out of his grip and cupped his face. "I never want you to stop."

He groaned suddenly, buried deep, and then his thrusts became frantic until he climaxed. She hugged him close as he shuddered and moaned, loving the heat of his skin and the heaviness of his hips against hers.

After a moment, he drew back and met his gaze.

"So that was lovemaking?"

"That was lovemaking," he said, tucking a strand of hair behind her ear. It was a sweet and lovely gesture that made her smile.

"How long before we can do that again?"

"After we marry," he said with a laugh.

Daisy pouted and drew swirls upon his chest hair. Her fingers drifted downward, intending to tease him until he changed his mind.

But he stopped her by slapping his hand over hers. "Or ten minutes, if you keep doing that."

"I'm done waiting," Daisy promised, kissing him deeply, so he was left under no illusions about the fact that what she wanted couldn't wait.

Chapter Fourteen

"You're scowling again," Daisy complained four days later, digging her fingers into Max's arm as they entered yet another ballroom together, but this time possessed of their great and wonderful secret.

"But not at you," Max promised, glancing at her tiny hand upon his sleeve and liking it there.

"Just as well," Daisy said, pouting just enough to make him want to kiss her lips and make her come again.

Max had no difficulty acquiring the special license to marry Daisy. He only had to work hard to keep the grin from his face tonight. They were set to wed tomorrow morning in her home. Everything had been arranged—witnesses, vicar, and wedding feast to follow.

He could not wait for tomorrow. For the wedding and an end to his bachelorhood. He wanted his family—Daisy and their merged households—all under one happy roof again.

The duke had written, demanding he present himself at the estate forthwith. He didn't yet know about Daisy, but Max would not go there without his wife by his side. Honoria still wrote to him daily, speaking as if their marriage was a forgone conclusion. The woman was nothing if not determined to become a duchess.

Max covered Daisy's hand with his, glad he did not have

to face the woman alone, or those little girls, either. "I had hoped this attending ball nonsense could be over and done with now."

"Hardly," Daisy warned. "I want to dance with my handsome beau. Flirt with him quite shamelessly, too."

"I do enjoy your flirting."

"I can always tell," she whispered, and then laughed. "Oh, Throsby, is it not a glorious night?"

"It most certainly is an improvement having you pleased with my company," he noted.

His minx grinned impishly.

They had arrived together tonight in his carriage, and no one had taken any notice of that fact yet. But it was a miracle they had made it through the front doors at all. What Daisy wanted, Daisy pursued. Currently, that was him, and more kisses and orgasms for both of them.

Things had turned dangerously heated between them halfway here, and he'd made his coachman circle the block once before they'd been able to alight. Not that Max minded being seduced constantly. However, he had promised Daisy that they would attend this ball and dance together. Their first and last engagement as a betrothed couple.

Not even the Duke and Duchess of Mamble knew about them yet. They were attending a different ball tonight, and Daisy hadn't had a chance to see her friend.

Following the wedding, they would enjoy a leisurely dinner with the Mambles in the late afternoon and share their happy news. Daisy, who still regretted her father was not alive to give her away, had asked that their wedding take place without any fanfare. Max had tried to change her mind but she promised that Gabby would understand her reasons. And then the fuss would die down and Max would settle back into life in Daisy's cozy little home. He was looking forward to moving back.

"I did like it better when I didn't have to dance and could simply watch you twirl about."

"Would you prefer to watch me dance with other handsome gentlemen on the occasion of my first and last public appearance as your betrothed?"

He thought about that and scowled. "No, I would not."

Her grin was decidedly smug. "Then ask me to dance, my lord."

"You're hardly going to refuse me," he murmured, enjoying their banter even as he nodded to Abelton, who smirked to see Daisy hanging on his arm. Abelton knew they were engaged. Max had asked him to stand up with him when they wed.

"You never know. I might have to," Daisy warned. "Other men might ask me to dance before you can, at this rate."

He almost laughed at the ridiculousness of her statement. Daisy had refused him nothing since their first kiss, and no other man would come between him and his future wife tonight or any other night.

They'd left squabbling and disagreements over nothing far behind. He let Daisy have whatever she wanted, like reading the paper first in bed this morning, and he'd only read it after she was done, sitting by her side and sipping tea. He was prepared to accommodate his woman in all matters just to see her smile at him. His future duchess deserved the best, after all she would have to endure. She'd be helping him manage his wards, their difficult mother, and the duke, too.

He turned to her and bowed deeply. "Miss Ellis, might I have the pleasure of this dance?"

She made a show of inspecting her empty dance card before graciously accepting, handing him the card and a tiny pencil to scratch out his name. He wrote large, taking up the entire card, before handing it back to her.

Daisy studied his signature and then tucked the card away in his pocket. "Something to show our daughters when they are old enough," she murmured.

She glanced up at him now with a playful smile and eased her gown off her shoulder. She still liked to play her little games. Always determined to tease him into a behavior meant just for her.

But he had a promise to keep right now and would not be so easily led astray.

Max led Daisy to the dance floor, and they passed Abelton, who smirked again because he'd always believed Max and Daisy were meant for each other.

They drew level with Miss Dawes, who regarded them steadily without smiling. Miss Dawes appeared not to be happy still, but Daisy only nodded politely. Though she had caught them kissing, Justine had not said a word so far. After tonight, he would not be so worried about the girl spreading rumors besmirching Daisy's reputation. But as ever, it was impossible to know what the girl might do.

Before the dance even began, Max couldn't help but twirl Daisy about the floor and pull her close to his chest. People stared. That was his intention.

"Now everyone has reason to look at us and wonder.

How long do you think it will be before they start whispering?"

"They already are," Daisy promised with a laugh. "But society has a short attention span. In a week, our behavior will be forgotten, and they'll have moved on to the next scandalous couple to gossip about. I wonder who that might be?"

Yes, people were whispering and pointing now. He released Daisy to take their places as the musicians began. "You're probably right about their attention being too easily diverted," he agreed, and suddenly wished society might make a larger fuss of their union, for Daisy's sake.

She'd been mislabeled a wallflower all season, on account of her lack of funds. On the eve of their wedding, she deserved to be thought a diamond instead. Although he had agreed about the small wedding, he wished it might have been more for her sake.

They'd never danced before but had no difficulty with the steps of their first set together. Max twirled about with Daisy and even enjoyed everyone watching him do it.

Daisy's cheeks slowly turned pink, though, under the strain of so much scrutiny.

He stopped dancing suddenly and pulled her out of the way of the other couples. He raised her hand to his lips and pressed a long kiss to her knuckles, as he held her gaze.

Daisy appeared startled. "What are you doing?"

"What I should have done the moment we arrived. I want no confusion or doubt," he promised. "I adore you, Miss Ellis."

He said it loudly.

Proudly.

"I love you," he said again, intending for everyone to hear.

Daisy swayed on her feet. Her eyes, though, rounded and filled with tears. "Since when have you become so romantic?"

"Only since the guardianship ended," he assured her—and the crowd. "I always thought your previous suitors were fools not to stand up to me to be with you. But I guess they valued funds more than love."

She beamed even as the crowd around them started to mutter about them, and loudly now, catching on that another bachelor had been well and truly caught in the parson's noose. But society had to know he married of his own free will. Not out of obligation or for money or because he'd compromised her.

He'd chosen to put love first, and always would.

"Oh, you beastly man. You turn nice and now I'm moved to tears over you," she complained, swatting at him even as he handed over a handkerchief.

A woman laughed at her complaint.

"Then cry on my shoulder if you need to. I'll always be here for you," he promised.

"You know, I usually only cry when I lose people I love, so I expect you'll not give me a reason to cry for a good long while."

"It will never be intentional if you need to cry over me," he swore, and bent down to seal his promise with a public kiss that made the crowd around them howl with outrage as well as encouragement.

Max no longer cared what society thought about him or Daisy. He was loved, and loved completely. It was all he needed. But every man knew that his worrying days were far from over when they tied the knot. Daisy, the minx, would be forever in his thoughts now.

Epilogue

Daisy folded her hands in her lap, covering up a book she never planned to read. She raised her face to the sun and smiled to herself. She was a wife, and that caused her heart to sing because it was Max she had married that morning.

There were still scandalous experiences left to enjoy, but her husband was the first and foremost on her mind now.

She could not wait to get her hands on him again. To entice, to tease, to kiss him at her leisure. The man was an addiction. A scoundrel who tried to be good. The more of him she got to know, the more about him she craved to discover.

A throat cleared, and Daisy opened her eyes.

"Ah, Miss Dawes," she murmured, smiling despite the perilous nature of her errand. "A pleasure to see you again."

Justine regarded her warily and then glanced around the square. "Miss Ellis. What are you doing so far from home?"

Daisy uncovered the book hiding under her hands. "Would you care to join me for a moment? It's such a beautiful morning for reading."

Justine's eyes fell to the book on her lap, which now bore a fresh cover of soft blue, courtesy of Throsby's talented valet. Justine, however, only frowned until Daisy flipped open the book to display Justine's handwriting within.

She sat down at her side very quickly. "I do often sit here in the morning."

Daisy closed the book again. "Yes, I remembered you telling me that, which is why I've come today. Throsby sent me here on his behalf." She set the book on the bench beside her but left her hand sitting atop it for a moment. "He assured me the book has not been read by anyone."

Justine turned, and her gulp was audible. "Have you read it?"

Daisy lifted her hand. "I did not."

Justine snatched the book from the bench and held it tight against her chest with a small but audible gasp of relief. "Thank you."

"I can only assume by your reaction that the contents of the journal are scandalous," Daisy suggested with one brow raised.

Justine did not respond.

"It would not have bothered me that you might have written horrible things about me or Gabby in there."

"It is not about either of you," Justine said firmly.

Daisy was relieved but also intrigued. "But it *is* scandalous?"

"Many would be shocked," Justine admitted slowly, gulping.

"Well, well, well, how interesting," Daisy said. "A shame I never knew this side of you before."

Justine fell silent again.

Daisy gave up the subject of the journal to speak of what she had come to talk to Justine about. "Miss Dawes, you might have some misgivings about my character, given a recent event you witnessed. Lord Throsby and I have formed a sincere attachment and we married today. No doubt you will believe your earlier suspicions about us were correct, but it was unexpected by both of us. However, our marriage is an event we've begun with great eagerness. I should not like gossip to mar what is most certainly a match made because we love each other deeply."

"I am happy for you both," Justine whispered. "He is a fine man, and you will never hear that I suggested entrapment."

"Good. He is indeed a fine man and overly concerned about my reputation in the face of what might seem to others as a hasty marriage. In a few days, we will be taking a trip into the country to visit his family." Daisy dug in her reticule and produced a key that she slid across the bench seat toward Justine. "When we are gone, and I think it should be for at least a month, should you ever need refuge or a moment to yourself, you are welcome to avail yourself of my townhouse."

Justine glanced at the key. "Why would I need—"

Daisy quickly cut her off. "It is clear to me that all is not well with you. I want to help."

"I don't need help," Justine said, and then stood. "Besides, there's nothing that can be done."

"Lord Brookes was never the man for you," Daisy promised, while wondering if that was the only cause of Justine's distress. "You deserve someone better than him. Someone who will stand by you, no matter the difficulty."

"There's no need to concern yourself with my future, such that it is," Justine whispered and then fled, headed back toward Lord Brookes and her sister's home, where she lived now, journal clutched to her chest. As furtive as every encounter of theirs had been in recent weeks.

Daisy looked down for the key—and discovered Justine had taken it after all.

She smiled to herself. Justine was a sly one indeed, and fast. She would not admit she needed help, but she would avail herself of it if need be.

Daisy sat a moment but decided that her coming here had achieved her goal. It must be awkward living with a newly married couple who did not like each other. She hoped Justine did not still harbor feelings for Lord Brookes. That would be too awful to bear.

If refuge was all the help Daisy could offer, then so be it. Perhaps Justine would have a chance to write more in her journal while there.

Daisy stood and headed toward the Throsby carriage, which was parked a short distance away. It was a relief to slip inside and be surrounded by a familiar conveyance.

She headed home, knowing Max would be waiting impatiently for her return so he could make love to her again.

Her staff, *their* staff, had gone above and beyond to prepare for their wedding day. As she'd suspected, they were all delighted by the news that she and Max would make a match.

When the carriage stopped, Max was waiting for her on the pavement. He entered the carriage scowling, though, instead of helping her out.

"What's the matter?"

"Nothing. But there's been a change of plan that I had nothing to do with," he said.

Max gave the driver instructions to head for Hanover

Square. That was where his town house was, but not where they were planning to spend tonight.

"Explain," Daisy demanded.

"It was decided by your servants after the ceremony we should live in a viscount's home. They sprung the decision on me only after you left, I'm afraid."

Daisy gaped. "The nerve."

"Yes, I said the same, and much worse. However, they were determined. They removed all your possessions while you were gone, and all the food too, and took care to inform the Duke and Duchess of Mamble and Abelton of the change of address for the celebration, as well. They even took the vicar with them! So there was nothing I could do by that point."

"Do they remember who they work for?"

Max caught up her hand and kissed the back of it. "A future duchess. They are determined you begin your new life in a certain style."

"Well," she said, huffing, and then kissed the back of Max's hand, as well. "We'll have to do something about them."

He snorted. "We'll probably increase their wages and give them all an extra day off."

She smiled at Max, and then laughed. "I'm glad."

"Ah, here we are. Hanover Square and Throsby House."

The carriage stopped, and Max leaped out. He turned back, his hand outstretched toward her. She gladly put her hand in his and allowed him to help her out of the carriage.

"I assume by your good spirits your meeting went well," he asked, threading her arm through his and leading her up the stairs, as was his right and her pleasure.

"As expected," she answered. "Justine has the key now, but I don't know if she'll use it while we are away."

"Well, if she does, it is a comfort to know she'd be the last person to arrange an assignation in your old bed."

"Or yours," Daisy countered. "There was something scandalous in that journal, I think."

"It's none of our business now," Max warned.

"Yes, I suppose that's true, but I cannot help but be a little curious." Daisy squared her shoulders.

"Ready?"

"I am."

"There'll be no going back. To your town house, I mean."

"I only want to be where you are," she replied, and grinned at him, and he only regarded her steadily. "Let us not keep those bothersome servants of ours and the guests waiting."

Max swept her off her feet and carried her into his home.

The entrance hall was awash with flowers, and the servants who greeted them had donned ridiculously excited grins. Max set her feet on the parquetry floor but kept her in his arms as he squeezed her tight. "Welcome home."

"Thank you," Daisy said, looking about eagerly. Throsby House was a great deal larger than hers had been and she could see herself living here very comfortably. However, Daisy experienced a slight pang over leaving behind her childhood home without a second glance. She'd had good memories of the place she'd grown up, and of her father while he'd lived.

But it was time to look forward, not back.

She grinned at the sight of the Duke and Duchess of Mamble in what must be the drawing room.

Gabby rushed over and hugged her tight and whispered, "What is going on? Why was Throsby carrying you."

"We are married," Daisy said proudly. "We are in love."

The duke must has suspected because he grinned, "Congratulations."

Gabby hugged Daisy a second time. "I can't believe you fell for Throsby!"

"Neither could I," Max said with a soft chuckle.

Daisy escaped Gabby and threaded her arm through his and smiled. Max made her happy.

"You'll have to tell me how this happened and soon." Gabby grinned. "Because I suspect I will not see you for several days, given how your groom is smiling at you."

Daisy giggled and glanced up at Max. He was looking rather delicious to her right now, too. Her devilish husband. "No, probably not."

He went to speak with the vicar, who had regarded her with the same stern expression during the ceremony as Throsby often had in the past. The ceremony had passed in a blur. She'd ignored the dire warnings of avoiding sin and other vices as she held Max's hand tightly, and when the time came, she said *I do* without hesitation.

Max was what she wanted, him and the challenge of keeping the frown forever off his face.

Throsby returned and pressed a light kiss to her cheek, and then whispered, "*Lady Throsby.*"

Daisy giggled.

She couldn't help it. She was deliriously happy. Throsby, Max, had made her dreams come true. She'd married a man who loved her. Who put her first.

"Well, my lord."

"Well, my lady."

She giggled again.

Throsby grinned. "Are you going to do that every time I address you by your title?"

"Well, I'm happy."

His arm went around her back, and he pulled her close. "As you should be, married to me."

He suddenly swept her up into his arms and spun them around, holding her tightly as she shrieked at the shock of Max doing something so impulsive.

She met his gaze and, to her surprise, saw bright eyes and a smile as wide as she'd ever seen on anybody. It quite transformed him. "Throsby!"

"Yes, darling?"

"You're so handsome when you smile like that."

He set her down on her feet and held her gently against him. "I promise to only show my best smile to the lady I love beyond belief."

"As ever you should, my lord," she whispered, before pulling his head down and claiming his lips with another searing kiss.

The series will conclude with Miss Dawes Takes a Rake, Book 3 in the Entangled Series

About Heather Boyd

USA Today Bestselling Author Heather Boyd believes every character she creates deserves their own happily-ever-after—no matter how much trouble she puts them through. With that goal in mind, she writes steamy romances that skirt the boundaries of propriety to keep readers enthralled until the wee hours of the morning. Heather has published over fifty regency romance novels and shorter works full of daring seductions and distinguished rogues. She lives north of Sydney, Australia, with her trio of rogues and a four-legged overlord.

Find out more about Heather at:
Heather-Boyd.com

facebook.com/HeatherBoydRomanceAuthor
instagram.com/heatherboydbooks
bookbub.com/authors/heather-boyd
goodreads.com/Heather_Boyd